THE HOUSE BUILT 'TWEEN THE BRANCHES

WILLOW WHITEHEAD | EMMA LOVEJOY
DANNI GRACE | ANNE J. HILL | MIA DALIA
HAILEY HUNTINGTON | ABRAHAM VILA
KARISSA RIFFEL | EFFIE JOE STOCK
ANAYIS DER HAKOPIAN | HANNAH CARTER
VANESSA E. HOWARD | K. DeCRISTOFARO
AUDRAKATE GONZALEZ | JULIA SKINNER
NATHANIEL LUSCOMBE | XANNA RENAE
SHERI YUTZY | DENICA McCALL

This is a work of fiction. Names, characters, mythical beings, places, and incidents are either the product of the authors' imagination or are used fictitiously in a completely fictitious manner in which all things were made fiction. Any resemblance to actual persons, living or dead or stored in a freezer somewhere, events, or locales, also, perhaps, in a freezer somewhere, is entirely coincidental.

Cover Art Copyright © 2024 Xanna Renae
All Story Rights Belong to the Authors

All rights reserved. No part of this book may be reproduced or used in any manner without the written permission of the copyright owner except for the use of quotations in a book review. For more information, address:
Editor@NightshadePublishing.com

First Edition October 2024
ISBN 979-8-9905539-1-0
ISBN 979-8-9905539-2-7

Published by Nightshade Publishing®
NightshadePublishing.com

THE HOUSE BUILT BETWEEN THE BRANCHES

Other Anthologies by Nightshade Publishing®

Through the Violet Redwoods
The Willow Tree Swing
Of Ink & Paper
Balloon Children

Other Works by Nightshade Publishing®

Down with the Prince - Xanna Renae

Stories

Beautiful Glowing Poison 🌿 1
I'll Keep Your Memory 🌿 2
My Friend, Wallabye 🌿 9
The Bird of the Night 🌿 24
*In the Woods 🌿 27
Song of the Forest 🌿 51
Untitled Poem by Abraham Vila 🌿 57
The Well at the End of the World 🌿 59
*Sacrifice Rock 🌿 85
Death Lies in the Wych Elm 🌿 91
*Demons and Dekkonali 🌿 94
The Roe Girl 🌿 118
*Revenge Song 🌿 127
*Haunted 🌿 129
Little Red Monster 🌿 146
Forest Gods 🌿 155
*The Breathing Woods 🌿 157
Moonrise 🌿 184
Trees 🌿 192

Content Warnings on Following Page

Content Warning

We understand this is a thriller/horror anthology, and that every story contains elements which are spooky or dark in some way, shape, or form. However, we still feel that we should ensure readers are aware of all the content in the anthology as some things may be disturbing and/or upsetting. After all, the point of reading is enjoyment, and we want you to enjoy all of the stories in our anthology.

Listed in alphabetical order, not story order.

- Animal Death
- Body Horror
- Cannibalism
- Child Abuse
- Death
- Forced Capitivity
- Gore
- Miscarriage
- Mental Illness
- Physical Abuse
- Rape/Sexual Assault
- Violence

Notes

The stories and poems are arranged much like one would find themselves walking through the woods. It begins with a thin canopy overhead, the pieces are lighter in tone. Then, as you walk further and deeper into the forest, the pieces grow darker and more grim. However, we do not leave you in the dark. There will always be a light on the other side of pain and sorrow. Waiting there for you to walk into it and bask in the warmth.

*You're not alone
in the woods.
You're never alone.*

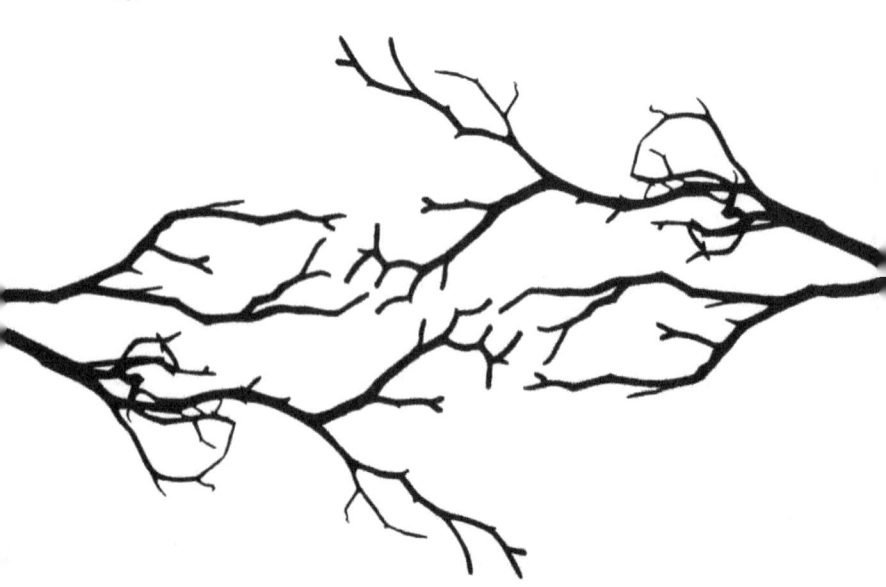

Beautiful Glowing Poison

Willow Whitehead

Mushrooms grow on my windowsill
    They spread up my walls
    They overtake my ceiling
They seal off my door
Beautiful
They comfort me as I drift off to sleep
It seeps into the cracks in my walls
It illuminates the holes in my floor
It soaks into the pages of my books
Glowing
Spores fill the air in my bedroom
They scatter over my clothing
They permeate my lungs
They spill out of my mouth
Poison

I'll Keep Your Memory
(I'll Wear it on my Skin)

Emma Lovejoy

The two children are strangers to me. They're running, and laughing, the girl chasing after the boy, trying to tag his arm. They're friends. Her hair is in long braids tied with pink ribbons. He wears wire spectacles that slide down his nose.

I welcome them.

They visit me often, now.

I've learned their names: the girl with the blonde braids is called Rosemarie, and the boy with the spectacles is called Remy. They are nine and ten summers old.

On sunny days, they walk through the woods to see me, with a picnic basket or chess board or books, and we three while away the afternoon together.

In the winter, they strap snowshoes to their boots and take long walks in the woods, tracking rabbits and noting the different kinds of birds they see. They come by often when they're on these walks. They sit, and rest, and talk, and then go back on their way.

In late summer, they spend the morning picking berries and then retreat to the shade when the sun is high and hot. They bring their pails of fruit and spend the hottest part of the day with me.

On a warm spring evening, they bring their friends after school. The boys play at sword fights with fallen sticks. The girls braid flower crowns or sit and practice needlepoint. I am glad to meet more friends.

I see them less often this winter. Remy says he is working at a shop in town. Rosemarie has a new baby sister she must help look after. It is harder for them to get away than when they were small.

Winters have passed. Summers have passed.

We have grown older.

Remy comes alone, after nightfall when the moon is bright.

He brings a lamp, and his little notebook, and by the lamp and the moonlight he writes. He tries lines of poetry out loud as he goes. When he finishes a poem, he always reads it aloud. The very worst of them, he tears out of the notebook and sets alight with the glowing end of a cigarette. Only he and I will ever know these unworthy works.

※

Rosemarie's hair is darker than it was when we met. She wears it up, tucked under a hat that she says is very fashionable. She is always very put-together: beautiful, and proud of her beauty. Remy is tall, now, and his voice has gone deeper. He still wears wire spectacles. It is very pleasant to listen to him read. My friends are nearly grown.

※

The moon is full and Remy has brought some other boys from school. They are bundled in coats and scarves, although it is not yet full winter. They drink brandy from a bottle passed from hand to hand, and talk of books they've read, and of the girls in town. Remy tells us he is in love with Rosemarie. No one is surprised.

I wonder what it would be like to be loved by someone like Remy. From his poetry, I think I know what it is like to be in love with someone like Rosemarie.

※

At Christmas, they tromp out to me through the snow to exchange gifts. Rosemarie gives Remy a stack of white handkerchiefs on which she's embroidered his initials in pale blue thread. The thread matches his eyes.

Remy gives Rosemarie a pair of fine apple-red leather gloves and a knitted hat of the same shade. It is the color of the hair ribbons she favors.

They've brought beautiful glass baubles for me.

※

They rarely arrive together anymore. One will appear and settle in to wait. The other will not be far behind.

Today, Rosemarie lays out a blanket to sit on, and Remy opens a book and reads aloud to us for hours. Rosemarie falls asleep while he reads, her head resting in his lap. He doesn't mind.

※

Today, they are very somber. They speak of politics I do not understand. Remy has brought a newspaper, and reads to us about the Kaiser and war in Europe. They share cigarettes. I miss the poetry. I think Rosemarie also wishes he would read poetry instead of the newspaper. She looks very sad all the time he is speaking.

※

Remy is anxious. He has been pacing since he arrived, and smoking one cigarette after another. He says he has no choice, that he's got to go, that all the young men have got to go. He swears softly and talks about duty, and honor, and the Germans, and Belgium. I will miss him, but he seems very sure of himself.

Rosemarie arrives, and he begins to repeat himself to her, but he has hardly started before she is weeping. He holds her and whispers all the words he has been rehearsing, and I try not to notice when he kisses her. She is still crying. They sit on the ground near me the rest of the afternoon, talking of Remy's plans and the letters he expects to receive when he is away, of what will be left for us here when he goes. They agree to come back again before he leaves so he can say goodbye.

Rosemarie's eyes are red from crying, and Remy says his mother is furious with him but his father understands. He promises to write often. They stay until night falls. He reads us poetry. He kisses Rosemarie and says how much he'll miss her. How much he'll miss me and this place that has been so special to them. He carves their initials into the tough skin on my body with his pocket knife. It is a rude thing to do, but I do not mind wearing their initials.

At last, when the moon has risen, he insists he must walk Rosemarie home, and so they go. I will miss him. I hope that Rosemarie will still come to see me when he is gone.

Rosemarie comes often. She sits and leans into me and weeps. She tells me rumors she's heard about the fighting in France. She reads me Remy's letters, and the little love poems he writes to her.

※

Rosemarie has stopped coming. A season has passed since she was here. Without her I have no news of Remy or any of the young men he introduced to me over the years.

※

I am worried about him.

※

I miss my friends.

※

I do not know how long it has been since she was last here, but I know Rosemarie's step at once. I am trembling with excitement as she approaches. It is raining, and she has rarely ever come in the rain. She is dressed all in black and carrying a black umbrella. She has been crying. She sits down beside me on the bare, wet ground, and begins to weep anew. She does not speak. I want to comfort her, but what could I do that would help? I do not know, so I do nothing. She leans against me and cries, and cries, and I hold her up.

At last, she gets up off the ground, sniffling. Her dress is wet and dead leaves stick to the skirt, but she does not seem to mind. She runs her fingers over the scar of their initials on my skin, and whispers Remy's name, and whispers "goodbye." I do not know if she means the farewell for me, or for him.

She says nothing more, only wipes her eyes and turns away from me. She walks quickly, and in moments, she has crossed my little glade and passed out of sight, hidden by the other trees.

I do not believe I will see either of my friends again. I am grateful for the scar they have left upon me. They will not be forgotten, as long as I stand here.

My Friend, Wallabye

Danni Grace

My friend, Wallabye, was gone. In the morning, I would follow.

I wasn't a very talkative kid. Some teachers might've said I was introverted. Antisocial, maybe. I didn't mean to be standoffish. It's just that whenever I talked to other kids, my stomach started turning, my hands would sweat, and I got too tongue tied to get a word out. My mom said I was just a late bloomer. Personally, I thought of myself more as a worm. Quiet, peaceful, and happy to wriggle in the soil by itself.

That's why I stopped going to soccer afterschool. We're supposed to meet at the park for practice. But something about getting yelled at by the coach and being taunted by the other girls for having a bad kick got really tiring after a while.

Instead, I headed the opposite direction. Near the school, if you go past the gas station and keep walking, the grass starts getting taller, and the buildings disappear.

Eventually, you'd reach a point where the field meets a line of trees that shadowed over any kid my size. Gnarled branches and twigs poked into brief view before being swallowed by the darkness inside. The leaves looked more like browned, withered crisps than the green, lively ones that would come to anyone's mind.

Those were the woods that sat on the outskirts of town. They didn't have a name, not that I knew of. Most people forgot the woods were even there. I guess that's easy to do nowadays, given there's just so much going on elsewhere.

The first day I sat by that treeline, it was about four in the afternoon. The sun was still pretty high in the sky, but a gentle breeze rustled my hair and tickled my skin. I plopped down in the grass, throwing my backpack to the ground. Grabbing my book from the bag, I prepared for what could be an hour or two of reading.

That's when I heard something snap.

I looked up for a moment, scanning my eyes over the area. I couldn't see far into the woods. It's a lot darker there than it is on the outside, as if it's a whole other world, far enough away so the sun can't reach it.

There was another snap. Leaves crinkled. Then, I heard it. Breathing. It was slow and light, like it didn't want to be heard.

I paused, sitting up. "Hello?"

No answer. I could still hear the breathing.

I raised an eyebrow. "You're not a very good hider," I

admitted blatantly.

At this, the breathing stopped suddenly. There was a moment of silence. Then, something shifted. With a voice so low you could barely hear it, it cleared its throat and spoke to me.

"I find it's hard to hide being my size," the voice replied, matter of fact.

"How big are you?" I asked.

"As big as the trees," he replied, it's voice deep and growly. "Sometimes, I hit my head on branches if I'm not careful."

"You're very tall then."

"Very."

There was silence between us.

"Are you just going to stand there?" I said, finally. "It's kind of hard to talk to people you can't see."

There was another pause. Then, through the darkness, something moved. A shape. Two hands, the size of a large bush or small sapling, came into the sunlight. I could see no skin, just black fur with strands of white sporadically growing in. The fingers, gnarled, did not take a definite shape, but were human-like enough to be identifiable.

"Whoah," I couldn't help but say out loud.

"It's okay," the voice said. "People are usually taken aback."

I stared at the inhuman hands. I'd never seen anything like them. I drew back, keeping distance from the voice and the mysterious woods it resided in. "Are you just a pair of arms or. . ."

"No," the voice said, unamused. "But I think it's best that I stay here."

I nodded, though curious still. "What's your name?" I asked.

"My name?" he replied.

"Yeah," I said, "what am I supposed to call you?"

"I don't have a name. Or a face, for that matter."

I gawked. "How could you not have a face? How do you talk and see and hear?"

"I do not know," the voice said. "All I know is that I am."

"All right." I huffed, moving on. By the minute, the figure grew less intimidating and a lot more confusing.

Continuing, I asked, "Well, then can I give you a name? A nickname?"

"You don't have to," the voice said.

"Well, I feel sort of silly calling you 'it.'" I admitted.

The voice didn't speak at first, as if pondering. Then, he replied, "Okay. What do you propose?"

I bit my lip, searching for the first name to come to mind. "Wallabye."

"Wallabye?"

"Mhm." I nodded.

"That's an unusual word."

"For an unusual person."

"Touche." Wallabye accepted my response, moving on. It almost sounded like there was a smile in his voice. "What is your name?"

"Jenny," I replied. "Jenny Mackentire."

Briefly, flashes of every safety presentation about "stranger danger" raced through my mind. They prodded at me, telling me I was incredibly stupid for introducing myself. I batted the worries away. Something about Wallabye didn't feel dangerous.

"What are you doing all the way out here, Jenny?" Wallabye asked. "Most people like you choose not to come around this area."

I shrugged. "I needed a place to go that wasn't soccer."

"Soccer?" Wallabye asked. "What's that?"

I raised my eyebrow. "You don't know what soccer is?" When I didn't get a reply, I explained. "It's a stupid game where you kick a ball around and chase each other. Sometimes people yell at you. Oh, and there's a net." I picked at a loose thread on my soccer jersey, and with a pluck, then a flick, I discarded the string into the grass. Stupid soccer.

"You don't seem to like soccer," Wallabye said.

"I don't," I told him. "The other girls are mean. They tell me I'm not good at soccer."

"Are you?" he asked.

"No, but it still hurts," I admitted. "I didn't want to play soccer in the first place. My mom made me."

Wallabye asked, "So these girls, are they mean to you often?"

I plopped down in the grass. It scratched my legs and crunched under my weight. "Sometimes," I said. "Depends on the day." I looked down at my lap and found another loose thread, this time on my soccer shorts. I pulled that one, too.

"This one girl, McKenzie, likes to pull on my braids." I gestured to my brown locks. "Another girl, Rachel, likes to trip me up while I'm dribbling the soccer ball."

"They don't sound very nice." He sounded genuinely concerned.

"That's not even the worst of it," I told him. "Sometimes, the girls tease me because I don't want to do the same things as them. This one time, they were going to go to the ice cream parlor after practice. I couldn't go because my mom was waiting up on me. So they said I was a coward and scared and a goody two shoes."

Wallabye shifted. I could hear something pop under his weight in the forest—maybe an acorn or gravel. "I am sorry."

"It's okay."

"If it makes you feel better," Wallabye said, his voice lilting upwards, "I know some people that also aren't very nice."

I looked up from string-picking. "Really?"

"There's a lot of things in these woods that are rather mean. They like to—" he stopped. "Well, they play very,

very rough. Especially with smaller beings, like yourself."

I tilted my head. "So they're like bullies?"

"Probably worse. A lot worse. When they get mean, they get hungry. And when they get hungry, they do a lot more than pull at your braids."

"That sounds awful," I said. "I'm sorry."

"I have gotten used to it," Wallabye said. "My only goal is to make sure I never become one of them."

"Well," I told him, offering a warm smile, "I can tell you that you aren't mean at all." It felt easier to talk to him than some of the girls on my own soccer team.

He laughed, suddenly, almost at a whisper or chuckle. "Thank you."

Over the next few weeks, I visited the woods. Soon, it became a staple of my routine. At first, Wallabye would watch while I read, and he listened to my stories. In return, he'd tell me a bit about the forest, like how if you were in the right place at the right time, you could see the full moon through the clearing of leaves in the sky.

The only time I didn't meet at the forest line was when I had a soccer game. While I could skip the practices, I couldn't miss the games without my mother wondering what was going on with me. Most of the time, I only came back home with a bruised ego.

One particular Saturday, though, the girls were feeling

cruel, McKenzie especially. Even though we were on the same team, she acted like I was her enemy. After the game, where I had scored the winning goal, she'd come up to me with her posse. She had her hands behind her back.

"Nice kicks, Braids," she said with a frown. There wasn't anything in her eyes that showed sincerity.

"Thanks," I said halfheartedly. "You too." My limbs felt stiff. I didn't want to spend another minute talking to her.

"Before you go. . ." McKenzie cooed, "I have something for you." She smirked. "A gift."

Before I could react, she threw her hands out from behind her. In her right hand, there was a jar filled with dirt. She flung the jar at me, and the soil came out from it, colliding and clinging to my hair. I screamed, grabbing at my straw-like hair, trying to pull the dirt from it, but the dirt just slipped through my fingers. I was grabbing so hard, I started to pull at my own hair, untangling my braids.

All I could hear was the girls' laughter as they walked away. They chanted my name, their voices more like the cackling of wild birds. My face burned and my stomach rolled. I noticed some of the dirt had fallen from my hair and landed on my jersey. I looked closer – there was a worm wriggling in the soil.

Darting my eyes back up at McKenzie, an idea crossed my mind. My vision was red as I honed in on McKenzie and her group of girls. She wouldn't make a fool out of me, not without me getting payback.

I started to march forward. "Hey! McKenzie!" I shouted. I plucked the worm from the dirt and carefully carried him in my hands. He needed to be alive.

McKenzie turned and rolled her eyes. She put her hands on her hips. "Haven't had enough of me, Braids?"

I ignored her. Taking the worm, I hurled it at her and yelled, "Go back to the swamp where you belong!"

I couldn't see if the worm made its target, but I watched as McKenzie went wide-eyed, her smirk falling, turning into a horrified scream. She started to flail her arms and kick her legs – surely the worm must've been crawling down her shirt. I couldn't help but smile to myself as I walked away.

That night, I was able to sneak out of my house after dinner. My mother worked the evenings, and so she wouldn't know I'd even been gone when she got back in the morning. I made the journey to the forest line, where I sat down, this time, bringing food with me: Microwaved chicken nuggets.

Wallabye appeared, as if I (or the chicken nuggets) had summoned him. A smile blossomed on my face upon seeing his shadow. It was good to be amongst a real friend again.

"Hello, Jenny," Wallabye greeted. His voice was monotone as usual, but I could tell by the light condition of his voice that he was pleased. "I thought you would not come today. You were not here earlier."

"Yeah, I'm sorry," I said. "I was at a soccer game."

"Oh?" Wallabye asked. "I thought you did not like soccer."

I nodded. "I don't, but I still have to go to the games, or my mother would start to worry about me."

Wallabye wondered, "You do not like soccer, but you still go because you're worried about your mother?"

"She works a lot," I said. I started to dig into my chicken nuggets as I talked. "I don't want her to know the other girls are picking on me because then she'd get upset. Not at me, but them and the coach. Then, she'd probably pull me out of soccer, and then she'd have to find a new shift at her job. She doesn't want me home alone because I'm too young."

Wallabye spoke matter-of-factly. "If I was in your shoes, I would just stop going to soccer."

"Do you have a mother, Wallabye?" I asked.

"I probably did," he replied. "But I do not remember her now. I spent most of my life taking care of myself."

"That sounds lonely." I swallowed my food.

"It is okay," Wallabye said. "I cannot miss anyone I cannot remember." He switched topics. "Were the girls mean to you today?"

I completely forgot I'd meant to tell him all about the game today. I grinned. "You'll never guess what happened today."

He listened quietly as I explained the events of the game. I told him about how I scored the winning goal, how McKenzie threw dirt at me, and then how I threw the worm at her shirt. He didn't say anything until I was done.

"I could never approach other monsters the same way you do," Wallabye said, sounding astonished.

I tilted my head. My mouth was full. "Other monsters—do you mean your bullies?"

"Yes." Wallabye's voice was quiet and resentful.

I swallowed more food. "Why don't you just talk to them? Or better, put a worm down their shirt?"

Wallabye replied bluntly, "Monsters don't wear shirts."

I rolled my eyes. "I was making a joke. My point is, why don't you stand up for yourself?"

"It's not that easy," Wallabye said sharply.

I folded my arms. "You're the biggest monster I know. Any monster would listen to you if you made your voice heard. Don't let them boss you around."

"It is a little more than that," Wallabye argued. He sighed. The action caused the ground to vibrate gently with his sharp, heavy breath.

One day, we sat together as I read him pages of my polka-dotted diary. He'd asked to hold it in his hands, flipping the pages, as if the texture were foreign to him. He'd been quiet all day, and this was the most he'd engaged with me.

"Are you okay?" I asked Wallabye.

"I am well," he told me absently.

I folded my arms. "Are you sure?"

"Yes, Jenny."

I paused. "I don't believe you."

"I promise, Jenny. I am okay."

From his hands, I gripped the diary and pulled it away. He reached out for it, but I held it to my chest.

"What's wrong, Wallabye?" I pushed. A thought came to mind, and I straightened. "Is it your friends? Are they being mean to you?"

"I don't want to talk about it."

I pressed further, "You can tell me anything. I'm here to help."

Wallabye paused, and for a moment, I thought he wouldn't say anything. With his tone harsh, he said, "You cannot come here anymore."

I drew back. "What? Why?"

"You just can't." His voice was laced with tension.

I stood up, brushing grass off my shorts. My heart sank. I'd pushed too far, and now he didn't want to talk to me anymore.

My pitch rose. "Did I do something wrong?"

"No," Wallabye replied almost immediately, regretfully. "It's not your fault." He sighed, clearly frustrated.

"Then tell me what's happened," I demanded, planting my feet into the grass.

Wallabye cleared his throat. When the words came, they fumbled from his mouth fast, as if there wasn't enough time to say it all. "Not all of the things that live in these woods are friendly, Jenny. Many of them hide amongst the trees and slink in the darkness, ready to pounce on something—someone—a lot smaller than them." He whispered like he was afraid someone would hear.

"It's okay," I reached out for his hand. "I'm here. I can take care of myself. If you're scared of the bullies, I can take care of you, too."

Wallabye laughed, but he sounded rueful, like he was pitying me rather than taking me seriously. "Maybe you can. I have no doubt your spirit is strong, but when it comes down to it, small limbs snap very easily." His words seemed to echo through the air.

We were both quiet. I looked at the ground and kicked a pebble, trying to keep back the lump coming up my throat. My face felt hot. I knew he was trying to keep me away because he thought he knew what was right, just like the adults did.

Finally, he broke the silence. "I'm sorry," he said. "But it's to keep you safe."

I folded my arms. Curtly, I replied, "I'm not leaving you alone."

Wallabye's voice hardened. "Yes, you are. I don't want to see you anymore."

"But what if—" I started.

He cut me off and gently squeezed my hand under his.

"I will be okay. Promise me you will not return."

I swallowed, then nodded reluctantly. He wasn't going to let me leave until I agreed.

After that, there was nothing left to say, and so I walked home.

Arriving at my small white house, I shut the door behind me. My mom wasn't back from work yet. Normally, I would've heated up chicken nuggets in the microwave, but I couldn't eat. All night, I sat in my room with a pit in my stomach.

I was never one to keep my word, and so the next day, I visited. The clouds were darker that afternoon, obscuring the sun. The wind picked up, crashing against the trees and chilling my arms and legs. The hairs stood up on the back of my neck. Like always, I sat before the woods, crisscross applesauce in the grass. I waited for fifteen minutes. Then thirty. After an hour, my cheeks began to grow red and my nose numb from the cold. Goosebumps collected on my skin.

Wallabye wasn't coming.

At first, I assumed he was mad at me. Maybe he didn't want to talk after the day prior. But that didn't seem right, either. He wouldn't just leave me. I came by again the next day. And the next. Every day that week, I visited, and Wallabye never came.

I thought about his bullies. I thought about the fear in

his voice. I thought about the monsters in the woods and the girls in soccer. They couldn't be very different.

That evening, I packed a flashlight, a sandwich, two water bottles, and a cookie in my backpack. Stopping in the kitchen, I took a piece of paper and began to write, explaining to my mother where I'd be going. Before I left, I passed the silverware display on the counter. I eyed the kitchen knife.

I wasn't going to need it, but something told me it wouldn't hurt to be extra cautious. I grabbed it and put it in my bag.

My friend, Wallabye was missing in the woods. A lot of things lived there, like wolves that chased little girls in red hoods and witches who lived in gingerbread houses. Whatever waited for me, I wasn't scared. Monsters were no bigger than the bullies at school.

The Bird of the Night

Anne J. Hill

Blood drips from the fangs of hedonism
    Seeping with a vampiric thirst for pleasure

Beauty that enchants the man
To wed the bird of the night
Who cries, "Give, give, give!"
Sipping on the ignorance of a nation
Spilling their blood on graves they built
In the name of Self-Comfort

The ground wails, for it loathes to be torn
By tiny coffins nailed in the name of Choice

The bird of the night is well-pleased

She sinks her teeth into intimacy

The House Built Between the Branches

And severs the bloodline at the throat

Desire with no cause, pleasure that bleeds
Intoxication of the man, gripping her flesh
Pleading to drown in denial; drunk on *happiness*
That wears a facade over gnashing of teeth

The life is in the blood she slowly drains
Until he is nothing but a husk
With veins looking for a new host
Death follows where life is dried out

To his knees, he falls, bowing in his chains
A puppet for the bird to sing her song into
To fill the spaces in his empty veins
His head droops, eyes glazed in slavery

He can now name the fangs piercing his flesh:
Pleasure without meaning, self above all else
He shouts into the void, "Meaningless! Meaningless!"
All hope has been sucked away

Until new blood spills out
Dousing the lies in red for what they are

The bird shrivels in the light of day

Choking on the life of her victims
She wars against the new Spirit in his veins

"Lift your head, oh you of little faith"
A whisper so violent it tears the veil
Between the husk of a man and
The God he drove into the grave

A slaughtering meant for destruction
Turned to build an army for the war already won
The husk of flesh is filled with a new battle cry
"Take heart, for the life is in *His* blood!"

Find a dramatic reading by Ben Garrett, on
Haunted Cosmos' Dusty Tome, Episode 47:
A response to Haunted Cosmos, Episode 6
"Vampires: The Life Is In The Blood"

Recommended to read at least once while listening to
"This My Soul" by The Gray Havens

In the Woods

Mia Dalia

For Chelsea

Childhood is a state of permanent helplessness, one the children themselves are perfectly unaware of. The moment they realize it, childhood is lost.

The woods are lovely, dark, and deep. Where was that from? A fairy tale? A book she'd read? Maybe a song? Vera couldn't place it, but the words haunted her. She had tried to find the loveliness in these woods, but time and again it stubbornly eluded her.

Truth was, these woods scared her. They weren't like the ones at home, the ones she grew up used to. These were the woods straight out of Grimm's fairy tales. This is what she'd always pictured Black Forest to look like.

The trees grew tall, bowing their heads together at the top as if conspiring somehow. If they were conspiring to obscure the sun, they'd have succeeded, for the sun had seldom penetrated their leafy canopy. As a result, it was never quite as warm here on any given day as it was elsewhere outside. Vera had learned to bring a hoodie or a light jacket with her whenever she ventured into the woods, whereas the rest of the time, just a T-shirt was enough.

Vera was small for her age, a skinny, coltish kid yet to attain the promise of her parents' easy good looks. She had her father's blonde hair and her mother's green eyes. Her skin freckled in the summer like someone threw sand grains across her cheeks. When she smiled, her face lit up, but she didn't smile very often. From an early age she was a frowner, a contemplator of things, a serious kid through and through. She liked the comfort of baggy clothes, treated clothes like blankets, in fact, which somehow only made her look skinnier. A kid that small could easily be dwarfed by others—things or people—and especially tall, tall trees.

It wasn't just that the trees were tall for she had seen tall trees before. The Redwoods, the tallest trees of them all, back when her parents worked in California. But those giants were majestic. She wasn't scared of them at all. They made her think of dinosaurs but in arboreal form. Her parents told her all about how old the Redwoods were, how special they were.

Her parents would know. It was their job. They were arborists. Tree specialists, really, but they preferred arborists. She did too. It sounded fancy. If she was going to school, she could imagine telling other kids all about it, all the things her parents knew about the trees, the way they helped the trees all over the world, all the places they've been to.

But no, she was homeschooled. With all the moving around their family did, it was deemed as the best solution. And she liked it too, liked being lost in her books, liked writing reports for her parents, liked doing all the research projects they'd task her with, but it did get lonely sometimes.

It all depended on where they were living at the time, really. If they were near other people, other kids, or if they were somewhere remote. Their locations varied—it made Vera the best-traveled kid she knew of—but she was usually able to find some joy out of each one.

Until now.

This place, these woods, confounded her. It was too strange, too—she searched her mind for she prided herself on her vocabulary and made sure to learn three new words every day with the assistance of her beat-up giant dictionary—foreign.

Technically, she knew, it wasn't. This was where her people came from. She had done a project on it, a family tree. Genealogy. Her mom's specialty. That's where Vera's name came from. It was pronounced differently here, though, not Vee-ra as she's always said, but Veh-ra. Another foreign thing.

Everything was different here. Vera didn't know if she was ever going to get used to it. The unsmiling people, the dark dark bread, and the red red soup they favored. The latter looked like blood. She knew it was just beets but couldn't bring herself to enjoy it.

There was something. . . genuinely unhappy about this place. It seemed like a place that happiness had forgotten or avoided. And sure enough, it steeped into her home too. Well, her temporary home. They never stayed anywhere too long.

Her parents were fighting more. The small house they were provided with at the edge of the woods didn't have walls thick enough to absorb the noise. And Vera couldn't deal with the anger and frustration she heard in their voices, couldn't deal with the way it made her feel. And so, she went to the woods, a place she'd normally come for solace. To sink her feet into the mossy leafy ground, to mute the world outside with the arboreal soundtrack of wind rustling through the branches and wildlife scurrying around, to feel at peace—that was her favorite thing, that was the loveliness the woods had customarily afforded her, the loveliness she failed to find here time and again.

Vera walked, her footsteps absorbed by the natural cushion of the forest's floor. It was quiet here, too quiet. The quietest woods she'd ever been in, she thought. No birds, no animals, but surely, they must be there, for what would a place be without them—a mere collection of trees? Not even good strong trees, as it happens. There was a blight upon these trees. Vera overheard her parents talk about it. Something the locals referred to with words Vera couldn't pronounce. The experts from the area couldn't quite explain it. That's why her parents were here, the world-renowned tree experts. If they couldn't fix it, no one could.

She thought it was strange that this is the place her father came from—he seemed so different from the local people. Happier, sunnier somehow. When they lived in California, he fit right in. Mom said he had surfer-boy good looks, tall, lean, wiry strong shaggy blonde, with a huge goofy smile on his face. Mom always had a smile on her face then too. Vera wished they never left California. But most of all, she wished they'd never come here.

It was impossible to keep track of time in the woods. Nature had different laws here. Vera had her trusty Swatch, but the plastic watch was no match for the trickery of the sun. Whatever hour Swatch told her it was, the tree-obscured sun had a different idea.

She left the house right after breakfast, but that morning her family ate really late. She remembered because she sat in the kitchen with a growling belly trying to concentrate on her book while her parents did that whisper-shouty thing they did in their bedroom. Eventually, they emerged and pretended like nothing happened, kissed her head, and made pancakes.

They couldn't fool Vera; she could see the residual sadness in their eyes, but, like so many things, it went unsaid. She couldn't ask and even if she did, they'd just say, it's complicated, which was their code word for 'We can't tell you.'

Vera would understand if they did confide in her. She was smart, smarter than most kids her age and even some older ones. She'd notice it whenever she had playdates before, whenever she made friends before—that slight but ever-present divide between her and others. She'd always tried to ignore it, for otherwise, she'd have no one to play with at all, ever.

And so, she made small compromises, didn't mention the books she was reading, the ideas she was having, played at their level. It was fine, really. It was better than having no friends at all, like now.

She'd seen some kids around, in a village near the woods and a small town further down her parents would go to for supplies, but those kids didn't seem friendly. They had pinched faces and unpleasant expressions like the miniature versions of the adults. Vera would rather be alone. But then, of course, she'd be alone like she was now in the woods, wishing for company.

She never worried about getting lost. From an early age, her parents had taught her how not to. She could read the woods like books. Vera could *easily* orient herself by whatever ambient light was available, whatever side of the tree had more greenery on it. There was a science to it. She loved knowing it. If there is a creek, you can always find your way to the water. In many ways, the woods were less confusing than the cities with all their twisted-up streets and incessant noise.

Once, Vera's parents took her to New York City and she thought it was the most confusing and confounding place she'd ever been to. She would have definitely gotten lost there had her parents not been with her.

They had fun then too. It wasn't just that sunny California elevated their moods. It was merely that this place had relentlessly depleted them. No wonder her dad left it as soon as he could. He studied in London, England; and Madison, Wisconsin. The latter was where he met her mom. The rest, as they liked to say it, was history.

A strange expression, Vera thought. To her, history was something that happened in the past, and her parents' story was still very much in the present. Only currently it existed in a sad and unhappy phase.

There was no family here according to her father. None left. Maybe they had all moved away like he did? Or maybe they died like her mom's parents? He never specified. He didn't seem to like it here either very much, though he at least spoke the language.

They probably would have never come here in the first place but for the fact that whatever was happening with the trees was a proper baffling mystery and her parents could never resist a good mystery.

How does a forest such as this turn into a shade of its former self? All the lovely birches and spruces and pines becoming but fragile ghosts of their former selves, zapped of vitality and strength?

The locals referred to it as taiga. It was the word for these great boreal forests. Vera knew from her parents that these boreal forests represented the largest forested region on Earth (approximately twelve million square kilometers), even larger than the Amazon. The mystery of the dying trees had to be solved as soon as possible before it affected more areas.

And it all started here, in what felt like the edge of the world or at least one of its darkest lesser-known corners. Now Vera was stuck here. She didn't know for how long. It could be—she searched her mental vocabulary—indefinitely. Now that was a scary prospect.

If she could only find some animals here, something lively, something to take her mind off her mind . . . Vera looked around. Nothing. Just trees and more trees, same as always. She walked on.

Her steady California-bought hiking boots made silent tracks on the forest floor. She thought of finding some branches to step on, if only to disrupt the oppressing silence. And then, she heard a sound.

She didn't believe her ears, at first, waiting for it to recur. Was there an animal here, after all? Maybe it was trapped and needed help. Heroic scenarios of saving some helpless furry creature fired up her imagination and buoyed her step.

The sound came again, this time unmistakable and distinctly plaintive. What animal would make a noise like that? Vera thought, moving faster toward where she believed the sound was coming from. Was there someone here? Another person?

Vera believed she had a reserve of heroism within her merely waiting for the right situation to prove itself. Perhaps it was a belief born out of reading too many comics. Since inheriting her Granddad's old collection, she's been through every book in it, back-to-back and more than once. They were silly, much sillier than the other *pictureless* books she was reading, but they spoke to something inside her and resonated with surprising potency.

She was practically running when she came upon a small clearing. She couldn't recall being there before. It looked as if the trees took a collective step back to give the ground some space. In the middle of it, there was a boulder, a sizable moss-covered rock upon which a person was sat. A very, very old person.

It took a moment to discern that it was an old woman. The clothes she wore were dark and shapeless and much too long. Her hair was gray and long and didn't look well-combed. She looked the way homeless people did in the cities. Unkempt and sad.

Vera knew from what her parents had told her that sometimes the homeless people had mental problems and were dangerous to go near, for they might be violent. But this woman didn't seem violent or dangerous. That sound she was making, Vera thought, had to be crying.

Maybe she was just lost. Vera's grandmother, her mom's mom, the woman she barely remembered, had dementia before she died which meant she forgot things and could get lost or harm herself easily. Maybe this lady was just like that, maybe she wandered away from her home and got lost.

Vera stepped up, cautiously. Up close, the woman had a distinct smell, like peat and spices. Her skin, what she could see of it, was impossibly wrinkled. Did people even get that old? Her hands were gnarled with long sharp nails and fat knuckles on bony fingers.

"Are you okay?" Vera asked, and then, remembering her manners, added "Ma'am."

The old woman stopped crying and looked up at Vera through the curtain of her long gray hair. Her eyes caught the light and for a moment looked golden before returning to a more pedestrian brown.

Vera realized that there was a good chance this woman didn't speak any English and repeated her question in the language she thought might be more easily understood. She knew she had an accent but thought she got the words right. She'd always had a good memory.

The old woman twisted her neck to the side as if regarding this intruder upon her thoughts. Vera thought she looked like a giant bird just then. The neck let out a series of popping sounds, *rat-a-tat*.

Up close, the older woman didn't look crazy or homeless, just very sad. Then again, Vera was no expert.

"I can't find my house," the woman said in a voice strange and creaky as if unused to speaking.

Oh, so she is lost, thought Vera. Well, that's okay. She could help her find her way. Vera even had a compass in her backpack, along with the other essential forest provisions like power bars, a flashlight, and water.

"Where do you live?"

"There used to be a house here. My house. And now I can't find it."

"Oh." How could that be? If there was a house here, surely Vera would have noticed, would have stumbled upon in on her treks. Besides, houses didn't just disappear, did they?

She thought of what her parents would ask had she misplaced something.

"When did you see it last?"

The old woman just shook her head. "I don't know. I was away for a while. A short while. It always waits for me, but now it's gone."

To Vera, it sounded crazy unless they were experiencing some sort of a communication problem. Things often got lost in translation. But surely, what this old woman was saying wasn't possible. She must have dementia, too. In that case, she would need help returning home and with other things. Vera was ready. She reached for her compass.

"You do not believe me, little girl?" the old woman asked suddenly, regarding Vera shrewdly.

Vera shrugged articulately, hoping it would pass for a noncommittal response along the lines of, 'no, how can I.'

"I can help you get home, though," she said brightly.

"But I am home. I need help getting my house back to me. It might have gotten lost."

Okay, now Vera was sure they were losing something in translation. The houses did not get lost.

"What is your name, little girl?"

"Vera," she responded automatically and then pronounced it again, the local way.

"Veh-rah. Ah. And yet you do not believe?" The old woman seemed amused.

Vera knew her name meant Faith but never gave it much thought. In fact, she thought Faith would have been a perfectly good name too.

"I believe you can't find your house," Vera said diplomatically.

"It gets old. It wanders off. But it always finds its way

back."

"What does it look like?"

"It is made of wood, small on the outside and large on the inside." Like the Tardis, thought Vera. "It has chicken legs and a fence of bones."

"Sorry, what?"

The old woman repeated the description. Vera was pretty sure she translated it right. It just wasn't possible. The woman had to be crazy, after all.

Oh boy. Vera wanted company, but this wasn't quite what she had in mind. Nevertheless, one must take life as it comes, as her father was fond of saying. She smiled her friendliest smile and offered the old woman some bottled water and a power bar. This was going to be. . . interesting. But possibly an adventure. And who could resist a promise of an adventure?

It wasn't until her walk home that it occurred to Vera that perhaps she should have been scared. It was an alarming thought, she turned it around in her mind, pondering it. She knew she wasn't scared at the time, but in retrospect, the old lady seemed just like a witch from the fairy tales she was raised on. Even the description of her house sounded vaguely familiar, but Vera couldn't quite place it.

Her parents prided themselves on reading to their baby girl the *proper* fairy tales, as they'd call them, not the Disneyfied versions. Brothers Grimm, Andersen, even Oscar Wilde. She understood that these stories were darker and scarier than the versions of them that became popular later. She watched the Disney cartoons and compared them against the originals. Her parents even had her do a report on it.

The witches were not kind in the stories of her childhood. They didn't offer gifts, only trades, and those always, always came at a high cost.

What if this old woman was indeed a witch? But witches tricked you. The old woman had asked for nothing of Vera, but what Vera offered, and even that was only a snack. She refused Vera's invitation to come to her house and meet her parents. All the older woman wanted was to stay there in the middle of the woods and wait for her house that was no longer there.

Was it some local thing Vera simply didn't understand? She resolved to ask her parents.

They were setting up the table for supper when she got home. It must have been later than she thought. She dropped off her backpack, unlaced, and took off her hiking boots, and went to wash up. By the time she was in the kitchen and dining room space, the food was all set out.

It was never much; her parents weren't great cooks. They ably put together meals out of packages and threw spices on top of those, or there were always sandwiches. They prioritized getting all the right amounts of fruits and vegetables, which wasn't easy in this place, and no one ever went hungry, but the lush family meals Vera saw in movies or read about in books were merely a thing of fiction to her.

The meal before them tonight was some version of a mac'n'cheese casserole with green beans. The cheese steamed and looked delicious, but from experience, Vera knew that the second-day leftover version of it congealed to a distinctly unappetizing shine.

There was an unaddressed tension around the table as if her parents paused mid-fight to sit down to eat. Vera chose to ignore it, she had, after all, something important to tell them.

She waited for them to ask her about her day and then launched into her story of meeting the old lady, omitting no details.

Her parents listened while chewing, occasionally interjecting with questions. She thought they seemed alarmed at first, and later, when she mentioned the house's chicken legs, their expressions turned incredulous and even slightly angry.

In the end, her father promised to go with her to meet the old woman. After all, he was the one who could communicate best with her.

That evening, while reading herself to sleep, Vera overheard her parents fighting once again. They were doing that angry whisper-shouting thing again.

"Well, looks like she inherited your imagination," her mother said.

"Or maybe just your tenuous grasp on truth," her father countered. It spiraled from there.

"You're calling me a liar?"

"If the shoe fits. . ."

"We're not doing that right now." Her mother shook her head. "Right now, we must consider that someone messed with our daughter's mind, someone at the very least deranged and possibly dangerous."

"They just talked."

"That's how grooming starts. I watched all those documentaries. First, they just talk. . ."

"This isn't TV," her father protested. "There's no grooming going on here. It's a different world."

"Don't I know it? I'm reminded daily of it."

"Why did you even agree to come?"

"Because you . . . you made it sound romantic. Second-chance romantic. So remote, it'll give us time for us, blah, blah, blah . . ." Vera could hear the bitterness in her mother's words.

"It *is* remote. We *do* have time," her father tried to soothe her.

"I hate it here." She sounded so angry and sad. Vera hadn't realized her mother was so angry and sad here.

"Well, I'm sorry, but this isn't forever. We'll figure out the problem, solve it and move on. We always do."

"You'd know all about moving on."

"It was *barely a thing*." Her father abandoned the whisper mode and went straight to shouting. "What was I supposed to do? You wouldn't even …"

"What? Feel frisky? After a miscarriage? Well, forgive me."

"Shh." Vera could imagine her father holding up his hands, palms out. "Let's bring it down, Vera might hear."

"I'm sure she's got her headphones on."

Vera didn't have her headphones on. She had them near and considered putting them on, but the conversation proved too intriguing not to overhear. She didn't understand all of it but made a mental note to look up what miscarriage was.

Her parents paused as if to gather their calmness like scattered marbles.

"It might be one of the locals playing a prank on her. Vera's such an impressionable kid," Father said, trying to sound reasonable.

"I wouldn't put it past them, these sour jagoffs."

"I'm looking forward to meeting this old woman and giving her a piece of my mind."

"Maybe we shouldn't have given Vera such a free reign with the fairy tales." Mother sighed audibly. "Maybe we should have incorporated more Disney."

"Absofreakinglutely not. The kid's all the smarter for understanding the world better."

"A world with witches in it? A world with dementia in it?"

"Yeah, though I don't know about the houses with feet."

"Not just any feet. . ."

There was a burst of quiet laughter for a moment.

"I remember those stories," her father said quietly, wistfully. "They terrified me as a kid."

"Well, tomorrow you get another shot at childhood," said her mother, and then their voices turned inaudible.

The internet was prehistorically slow around here, and you could all but forget about cell phone reception. Vera got used to looking up the things she needed in books, the old-school way, as her parents would call it.

She stayed up half the night looking things up in her dictionary and her volumes of fairy tales and folklore.

Learning about miscarriage made her sad; she could have been a big sister. It was difficult to imagine. She'd been an only child for so long. And then she finally found the house with funny feet and its owner who owned it and learning about it took over all her other thoughts. Baba Yaga—now there was a witch to end all witches. So scary, so wild, nothing at all like the ones from cartoons.

Vera fell asleep wishing that the old woman she met was indeed this witch of fairy tales and not just a senile local.

The following day Vera set off for the woods with her father. She'd packed her trusted backpack full of provisions. She even made peanut butter and jelly sandwiches—her only specialty—since it seemed like more of a proper meal than the power bars.

They walked and walked and, though she was sure they were going in the right direction, she struggled to find the same clearing again. By the time they came upon it, hours later, it was empty.

"There's no one here, pumpkin," said her father. She loved when he used her childhood nickname, but right now, she felt too disappointed to notice small pleasures. Where was the old lady? She said she'd be here. It must have been a prank all along. Vera felt stupid, just another dumb kid falling for a cheap trick.

Her father must have noticed. "Don't worry, kiddo, we all get the wool pulled over our eyes now and again."

She wasn't familiar with the expression and had him explain it.

They sat down and had a picnic in the shade of the tall birches. Her father complimented her sandwiches. There were apples too and some bottled water to wash it all down. It was nice, very nice, would have been perfect even, if not for the circumstances. If not for the lie.

Vera told herself she wouldn't go back to the clearing, but the next time she was in the woods, she found her feet carrying here there as if they had a will of their own.

And sure enough, once she got there, the old woman was there.

Vera told herself she wouldn't act like a stupid kid anymore, wouldn't be taken in by a trick. But then, the old woman looked so sad.

"Didn't find your house yet?"

"No. It hasn't come back."

It was strange how reality could be altered by the circumstances. Now that she was here near this old, sad, strange-smelling woman, it didn't seem like a trick at all. In fact, it seemed pitiful in a way.

"I brought my father here, but you were gone."

"I don't care for strangers."

"I am a stranger," Vera countered, proud of this statement and its quick logic.

"No, I know you. I know all about being a little girl who is all alone with only stories for company and no power to change things."

Vera had to think about that. She wasn't sure she translated it right.

"How do you know?" she asked.

"Little girl." The old woman's face-wrinkles rearranged themselves into something like a smile. "Do you think I was always this old?"

Vera said nothing. She was a smart kid, too smart for

her age, but some things, like a child's concept of time and age, are unalterable by book learning. It was, to her, almost entirely unfathomable that the ancient-looking woman before her was ever a girl.

"I tell you what," said the old woman. "You help me find my house. and I will teach you some things."

"My parents teach me things all the time."

"Not like what I can teach you, little one."

Vera considered this. It seemed like an easy deal. Why not help? She'd either be humoring and providing company for a senile lonely old lady, which seemed like a good deed, or she'd be trading a favor with a potentially all-powerful witch in exchange for some secret knowledge?

"I'll help," she said. "How do I help?"

"Well, my house does like little girls."

It took Vera some time to figure out that she was essentially being used as bait, but she found herself curiously unafraid. It was almost as if the forest had its own logic, its own rules. No one knew them better than the old woman and under her protection and charge, Vera felt safe.

She felt less like a kid, more like an adventurer. A heroine of her books, not just a reader of them. Vera spent every free moment in the woods now, all the while talking with the old woman, learning from her. The language barrier was dissipating with every day, her grammar was getting surer, her vocabulary was expanding.

Her father noted the improvement and attributed it to her studying, and, in a way, he was right. Vera was studying every day, first with her books and then with the old woman in the woods.

She already knew all there was to know about trees, but now she was learning about the rest of the forest, every plant, every mushroom, every grass held its own secrets, had its own uses.

It was a world unto itself, and like an optical illusion, once you saw it, you couldn't unsee it. At last, she understood her parents' love for trees, the way they must have seen the woods. Lovely, dark, and deep indeed. But not a place to fear. Never that.

Vera knew the old woman's house was responsible for what was happening with the trees here. It was just mischief, albeit a very dangerous one. She knew once the house came back, all would be well in the forest once again. She also knew it would mean her parents would have no more business here, and they'd have to leave. It was difficult to imagine leaving here now.

When Vera finally got the courage to ask the old woman directly if she were Baba Yaga, she received no direct answer.

"If there is a woman who doesn't conform to the rules of society, who knows more and accommodates less, she shall always be branded a witch. No matter what world, no matter what time."

It seemed cryptic, but Vera thought about it a lot until it started to make sense. She decided to become such a woman, she decided she wanted such power. She didn't want to secretly cry at the kitchen table at night like her mother or forget her entire life and die helpless like her grandmother. Better to be a witch.

The more power Vera felt, the easier it was to navigate the woods searching for the house. Eventually, she felt like she could call it, and it would come. And so, she did. And it did.

It was just as described and, after all this time of half-believing in it, it seemed surreal.

The house was more of a wooden hut, its chicken legs giant and powerful looking. The chimney was smoking. It even set up its own fence and it was indeed made of bones. For all outward appearance, the house seemed apologetic for taking off.

There was no entrance that Vera could see. "How do you go in?" she asked.

"Ah," said the old woman, "House, turn your back to the forest, your front to me."

The house did a sort of rotating pirouette, strangely elegant if precarious.

Now there was an entrance, creaking open invitingly.

It didn't appear menacing, or maybe it did, and Vera simply felt no fear. This new fairy tale reality she inhabited these days proved impossible to resist.

There was a large vessel that looked like a giant set of a mortar and pestle that appeared now beside the old woman. And a broom.

"A broom?" Vera smiled. "How very traditional."

"Not just a broom, my girl. Only a madwoman would travel on a broom—how horribly uncomfortable. What an idea. Now this. . . this is a proper way to travel."

With that, the old woman climbed into the vessel and demonstrated its aerodynamics while using the pestle as a sort of an oar. The broom was used to sweep behind her leaving no trail. Strange, but no stranger than the rest of it and thus, perfectly appropriate.

"So, wait. You had this all along? You could have just flown around and found the house anytime?"

The old woman shook her head. "There's an expedient way of doing things and the right one," she said. "We did this the right way."

Vera had to agree.

The old woman landed her flying vessel and climbed out of it. Already she seemed stronger, more energetic. There was less gray in her hair, Vera thought.

She took Vera's hand, and together they walked toward the house that lowered itself creakily to meet them.

Song of the Forest

Hailey Huntington

My first memory was Papa telling me not to go into the forest.

"There are strange tales about what happens among the trees, Evelynn. *Stay away*."

For years, I'd faithfully obeyed Papa. There were times when I hadn't dared to even go outside—the forest seemed so wild, branches raging in the wind, shadows lurking among the leaves. I'd stayed in our yard, the splintered wooden fence a barrier between me and the trees. I'd stayed safe and content in the open, grassy meadow.

Then I heard the music.

It was shortly after my tenth birthday. Kneeling on the lawn, I twisted dandelions together into a chain. The forest was quiet, oddly so. I glanced over at the edge of the trees and watched squirrels scampering about. They chattered at each other, squabbling over nuts and making me giggle. The trees had never seemed this tame before.

The flowers slipped from my yellow-stained fingers as I continued to watch the forest. Slowly, I inched closer to the fence for a better view of the squirrels. They were so amusing, darting up and down the trees, their cheeks bulging from nuts.

A low, rich sound filled the air, breaking my attention away from the squirrels. It sounded like a piano. A frown crossed my face. We didn't have a piano. We didn't have any neighbors. Where was the music coming from?

The song grew louder, its notes soaring high before dipping low once more. I found myself on my feet, leaning against the fence toward the forest. Closing my eyes, I let the music wrap around me. The song made me ache—I felt like crying and clapping at the same time.

Papa's boots thumped on the cabin steps behind me. "Evelynn!"

Opening my eyes, I tore myself away from the music and turned to him.

His face was stern, his thick black eyebrows furrowed. "Come away from the fence. Now."

Ducking my head, I walked over to Papa. He rested a heavy hand on my shoulder. "Stay away from the forest. I've told you this before."

"Yes, Papa," I murmured as he guided me inside. The door locked behind us with a click.

For the next several weeks, Papa forbade me from leaving the house. The song still swirled in my mind. Even inside the cabin, I could still catch snippets of it sneaking through the wooden boards. When I woke up, it greeted me. While I did chores around the house–sweeping the worn oak floor, washing the tarnished silverware, dusting the cluttered bookshelves–it kept me company. As I fell asleep, it sang me a lullaby.

I never told Papa about what I heard.

Soon, I found myself humming along to the music. Papa wasn't around to notice and be displeased. The song felt fuller with my harmony—like I was the missing piece.

Finished with my chores, I sat in front of the single cabin window, staring at the forest. Ever since I'd heard the music, the woods had seemed calm and gentle. The branches no longer raged. The shadows I used to see were gone.

The music grew louder. Longing welled up with me as I closed my eyes. Oh, how I wanted to go find where the music came from. Who played the beautiful song? I had to know. The music was a part of me now.

It was dark when Papa came back. The moon hung over the forest, the trees glimmering in the moonlight. "Evelynn, come away from the window," Papa ordered as he sat down at the table. The thin chair legs bowed under him. I took my place in the seat opposite. Between bites of stew, Papa spoke. "You can go back outside tomorrow. But you must remember the rules. Do you understand?"

My heart pulsed against my skin. I swallowed as my throat went dry. "Yes, Papa." I would remember the rules, and I understood them. But I did not promise that I would keep them.

The music filled the cabin as we ate.

It was windy the next day. While the rustling branches had at one point scared me, they now complemented the song—percussion to the piano's melody.

Focused on the music, I crossed the grass to the fence. I knew that the song came from somewhere beyond the trees. The grove looked so welcoming. Surely it wouldn't hurt to go look for the piano.

The memory of Papa's stern voice clashed with the song, creating a terrible dissonance. Splinters dug into my fingers as I gripped the rail.

Before I could change my mind, I slipped over the fence, entering the woods. Fallen leaves crumbled under my bare feet. The forest was quiet—there were no squirrels, birds, or deer—but the music was still there, drawing me deeper and deeper.

Soon, the forest had wrapped around me entirely. I didn't know which way led back to the cabin. But I hadn't found the piano yet, so I wandered further in. The trees grew larger and thicker, moss and vines snaking around their trunks. Leaves blotting out the sky. A cool breeze whispered against my skin. But I was not afraid. The music was with me, notes rising and falling, twirling like a dance.

Growing louder, the melody spurred me on. I broke into a run, brushing aside ferns. The beats of the music echoed that of my heart as I hurried toward the song.

Suddenly, the music was gone, and I stepped into a clearing. In the center was a gleaming black piano. No one sat at the bench. I held my breath as I walked up to it and rested my fingers on the keys. Then the song spilled out of me.

I'd never touched a piano before, but somehow I knew how to play. The melody soared around me, filling the forest and wrapping around me. Eventually, I slowed down and let the notes fade away.

A branch snapped behind me. Turning around, I saw a lady dressed in a gown reminiscent of leaves and lavender. Tears dripped down her cheek. "You've come home."

"What do you mean?" My voice held only curiosity, no fear. The woman's words carried the same cadence as the music, soothing any apprehension. Surely someone who echoed the song couldn't be bad.

"Only the children of the forest know its song and can play its instruments. Years ago, a baby was kidnapped. We had no idea what happened to the child. But now"—the woman gently cupped her hand against my cheek—"the forest has brought you back to us. The piano is yours. It's been here all this time, waiting for you to come home."

The melody rose up once more, the forest confirming the story. Peace settled in my heart. I looked up at the woman and smiled. "Will you play the song with me?"

Abraham Vila

January nights are cold and I can see the rain through the windows.

The branches moving along, the owls singing their song.

I wrote those verses tonight. Such delusion,
such vivid images around my head but just that,
meaningless words
sang from the nymphs in the darkened forest. A splendid vision, certainly,
but a mere vision after all. A phantasmagoria.

I wrote,
while your light caress uplifted my tears
followed by the beckoning moon,
while a myriad of stars overlooked.

And you were not here,

but far behind the branches. You remained inside the forest. With them.

January nights are cold and I just can see the rain through the windows. While I see your soggy eyes

there in the riverside.

Your selkie spirit never forgot its skin and you went away when March came.

I wrote the verses tonight. My mind flew away, stealing my senses.

Stealing your touch.

And I just walk over dead leaves.

But, alas, these words

and the soft tip of your fingers were just a dream,

a vision,

a phantasmagoria.

If you are not here,

may the water let me be by your side.

The Well at the End of the World

Karissa Riffel

River Meadows had always thought her name sounded too fairytale. In school, it had made her an irony among her classmates, all of whom had sensible names like Katie or Jennifer—names for people who were destined to live in Ottawa Valley forever, taking over family businesses or becoming farmers or loggers. But who was she kidding? That was still going to be her fate, no matter what her hippie mother had named her.

"Will that be all, Dave?" River asked her customer. The cottagers and tourists from the city had long since closed up their lakefront properties before the weather turned, so most of the clientele at their convenience store were locals now.

"You hear about that stray black dog on Highway 58?" he asked. She shook her head. "Bad omen, some guys were saying."

River's dad came out from the back office, boots squeaking on the ancient linoleum. "Really?"

"I don't know. . . I think that's just an old superstition." River handed the customer his change.

"Remember when we got caught at the hunt camp in that blizzard?" her dad said to Dave.

"Jimmy said he saw a dark colored wolf, eh?" Dave replied.

River's dad looked at her. "Exactly."

She rolled her eyes. When it came to local legends, Joe Meadows was a repository of information. The Meadows family had lived in the valley for generations, and he was always coming back from hunting trips with a new tale he'd heard from his friends or a story about something strange that had happened to him in the woods.

"Thanks, Joe." Dave waved goodbye then nodded to River.

Just as the customer left, Bellamy walked in. His brown curls plastered flat to his forehead from beneath his cap, and rain speckled on his coat's shoulders. Outside the storefront windows behind him, mist gathered in the valleys of the foothills of the Laurentian Mountains. Most of the trees had lost their leaves by now, turning the slopes a mix of rich evergreen and burnished bronze. Bellamy worked at one of the logging camps on the other side of the lake. Hours were long this time of year, and the work was exhausting. They'd barely seen each other all month. But maybe that was for the best.

"Ready?" Bellamy grinned and leaned his elbows over the counter, smearing the glass she'd just cleaned. River wrinkled her nose but said nothing; he looked too happy today to ruin it—and that didn't happen very often. His step-dad made sure of that.

She checked the time on her phone, which was about all it was good for with the spotty service out here.

"Just let me finish up here in the office. Then you kids can go, and I'll work the counter." Her dad disappeared back into the office.

River busied herself straightening counter displays that didn't need fixing. She felt Bellamy's gaze on her, steady with a weight it never used to carry.

The two of them had been best friends since they were born. Or maybe it had really started before that when their mothers had both found out they were expecting within the same week, both of them craving ketchup chips for their entire pregnancies. Bell had always been her one constant outside her family when her mom died of bone cancer when River was nine. And River had been there for him when his parents split up and his mother got remarried to the biggest jerk in the valley.

Bellamy fiddled with one of the lighters for sale on the counter, spinning it around and around in his hand. She snatched it from him and put it back in its slot. He blushed, absently rubbing his fingers together where their skin had touched. Suddenly she felt bad for acting so irritably with him.

He glanced at the closed office door and lowered his voice. "Have you told your dad that you're leaving next month?"

Now it was her turn to blush. "No."

"The longer you wait—"

"I know." She swallowed. Her dad would need time to find someone to help run Meadow's Convenience and Gas, but she just couldn't bring herself to tell him yet. She hadn't even meant to stay past the end of the summer.

"Make a wish."

"What?" she asked.

Bellamy gestured to her throat where the clasp of her necklace had fallen to the front. "You have to wish."

River closed her eyes.

Maybe it was crazy, but River had always thought the forest could hear her. Not the way humans could, language and sound waves, but some days when she walked in the deepest part of the bush where even the birds seemed to fall silent, she was certain something was listening. Those times, she imagined the trees knew all her secrets, even the ones she couldn't bear to say out loud.

Secrets are stronger than anything, her father always said, *even magic*. If only that were actually true.

The damp, mossy scent of wet earth rose around her,

and the crunch of her boots shattered the quiet. It got dark when you went this deep, even in the daytime. It was getting late, and she would have to double back soon before the sun set, but she needed to get out here today. Needed the quiet and the solitude.

It was this past summer when everything had changed between her and Bellamy. They had just graduated high school, and the world seemed so very wide. River wanted to get out of town, move to Ottawa, maybe take some college classes. Bellamy would get a job logging and save up for his own place. His stepfather yelled a lot, and that was putting it lightly. For most of their high school years, he'd spent more time at River's house than at his own. The night everything had changed, they were hanging out on the dock of her parents' cottage, drinking beer and counting stars. The cool night had driven them together, huddled beneath the only dry towel they had between them; they couldn't bear to go inside yet, not when the day had been so perfect. It was then, in the midst of bursts of tipsy laughter and familiar stories told sleepily in the dark, that Bellamy had kissed her.

Or maybe it had been her who'd kissed him. River had played the moment over and over in her mind so many times that she couldn't recall it properly anymore. Only the breathlessness of it, the way he'd held her so tightly, his hands warm on her bare back—the way he'd felt so solid and steady, just like he'd always been, only charged with some other-worldly heat he'd never had before. The towel had fallen from their shoulders and her fingers had gotten hopelessly tangled in his hair before they finally pulled apart. River ran back to the cottage, her bare feet catching on the exposed roots. When morning came, neither of them mentioned it. A day passed and then a week. Soon it was easier to pretend that it had never happened at all. Everything could go back to normal.

Then Bellamy had started dating Emily MacDonald, the sheriff's daughter and the prettiest girl from their class. And that, it seemed, was that.

Now, in the autumn woods, a chill prickled over her skin. River stopped, glanced around, and frowned, a cold, pitching feeling settling in her stomach. She'd gone hiking in this patch of the hills a million times, but just now she didn't recognize where she was. She stopped near an unfamiliar boulder to get her bearings.

Suddenly, a stone shifted beneath her.

She jumped up. It wasn't a rock at all; it was a stack of rocks in a rough circle, placed there at some point by human hands. A well?

"What's a well doing all the way out here?" she murmured to herself. Early settlers maybe? She glanced around for the remains of a house, but saw nothing. She peered down into the well to check if it still held water, but all she could see was endless black. Rusted coins had been jammed in between the stones. Sometimes settlers used to do that to the tree trunks to protect themselves from forest spirits, but she'd never seen it like this before. Maybe it was a similar sort of superstition. Maybe this was a wishing well. All this time and she'd never stumbled across it before.

A smile settled on her lips. This was the great thing about the forest; no matter how well you thought you knew it, it always held surprises. River fished around in her pocket for a coin then clutched it in her palm until she could think of a good wish. Then, she held the coin over the well, closed her eyes, and dropped it in.

A shadow fell over the woods, and a frigid wind stirred up her hair, stinging her bare hands and face. It rustled in the brush like footsteps. She whirled around, her heart hammering. There was nothing there.

Her skin flushed with a prickly sensation of unease. The boughs above creaked in the wind like doors in an abandoned house. At her feet, the dead leaves leapt into the air and swirled around her legs, as though animated by a ghost. The shadows deepened, and River's unease slowly morphed into fear.

It was close to sunset, but it wasn't that late; it shouldn't be this dark. Another gust hit her full in the face, roaring so loud she could almost imagine it had whispered, "Thank . . you. . ." Just as quickly as it had come, the wind died, and the shadows of the forest returned to the milky light of an overcast afternoon.

Still shivering, River checked the tiny compass on her watch face and started back down the slope. That would at least take her in the right direction. Mentally, she kicked herself for getting so turned around this close to sundown. In late October, exposure was nothing to mess with. And she didn't have to look at her cell phone to know that there was no service out here.

To her left, something black streaked past. It was too fast and small to be a black bear, but she quickened her pace anyway. There were a lot of animals she didn't want to tangle with in the dark.

When at last she found her rusted 1991 Ford Ranger where she'd parked it on the dirt road, the world had turned the deep blue of twilight. Her body went limp with relief as she climbed into the cab and blasted the heat. Here, her fears seemed silly. It was easy to imagine the voice on the wind had only been her imagination, the darkness just a stretch of passing storm cloud. That was right. And surely that animal she'd seen was a deer. It was mating season, after all.

So River drove the familiar, winding road home, leaving the forest to keep its secrets.

River swore she could feel the heat of the flames even from here. By the time the call had come in the middle of the night, it was already too late. The flames had consumed most of Meadow's Convenience Store, and the rest of it was sure to follow. River and her dad stood across the street while the fire department secured the area to make sure there wasn't another explosion.

Her father stared stoically at the inferno, his face lit up an unearthly gold. They had insurance, of course. But River knew that's not what he was thinking about. He was remembering when he and River's mom, Deborah, had met working at the store; remembering how they'd saved up and bought the place a few years after they got married. So much of River's mother was in those walls. Her childhood. Everything.

"Riv!" In the indigo of pre-dawn, Bellamy was jogging towards them, a fire helmet dangling from one hand. His face was streaked with soot, and his thick fireman's jacket hung open. "Are you okay?"

Suddenly she was not okay at all. Tears spilled down her face before she could stop them, her breaths crumbling into sobs. He hooked his free arm around her shoulders and pressed her to his chest, her face buried in his neck. She clutched the back of his jacket in her fists, smoke and gasoline burning in her nostrils.

"What if you'd been in there?" he whispered as though to himself.

"Bellamy! River!" Emily MacDonald, Bell's girlfriend, jumped out of her car wearing pajama pants, her blonde hair flying loose.

River hadn't even noticed her car drive up. She pulled away from Bell, wiping at her eyes, though she knew she was only smearing soot on her face.

"I can't believe this." Emily threw her arms around River. "I'm so sorry."

Numbly, River returned the hug, words seizing up in her throat. "Thanks."

She and Emily had basically nothing in common, but thirteen years in the same class had a way of making anyone friends.

Emily released her and turned to Bellamy.

"Em, you shouldn't have come." His voice was strained.

"Why are you even here?" She pressed a hand to his cheek. "I thought you were still in training. Are you being careful?"

"They needed everyone they could get. I wanted to come."

She let her hand drop and glanced at River.

He caught Emily's hand, and she smiled back weakly. "Yes, I'm being careful. They're not letting me do much anyway. I better go back though."

As though finally shaking himself from his stupor, River's dad came over to them and shook Bellamy's hand. "Thank you, son."

"I'm sorry about this, Joe."

Bellamy walked back toward the blaze, and River went to

stand beside her dad. She looped her arm though his and held him close. "We're gonna get through this," she whispered.

He touched the back of her hand, but said nothing. Emily stayed, which maybe shouldn't have surprised her, but it did—although she was probably there more for Bellamy's sake than River's.

They stood there until the sun came up. The fire fighters had quelled most of the flames, and the store had been reduced to a blackened shell with the pieces of its frame rising up like a skeleton, grotesque against the pastel painted sky.

By the time day had arrived, the empty lot across from the store was full of cars: friends who had heard the news, neighbors driving by.

"I heard a few people saw that black dog yesterday," said Rick, who owned the mechanic's down the road. "Coulda been a sign, eh?"

"You don't really believe that old wive's tale, do you?" Emily replied, raising an eyebrow.

"I'm just saying. Someone saw it and then this happens."

River frowned. The customer in the shop yesterday had told her about it too. Of course that didn't mean it was anything more than a stray dog, but her mind went to the animal she'd glimpsed in the woods. It had been about the right size for a dog. Normally she didn't give much credence to superstitions like that, but it did seem like an odd coincidence. And with the strange shadows at the well—

River's heart lurched. The well. Her wish. With everything, she hadn't even thought about it until this moment:

I wish I never had to set foot in the store again.

"No. No way."

"I'm serious, Bell. And you know I don't normally go in for stuff like this."

Bellamy stood looking at the well. Despite the fact that River had hiked for nearly an hour yesterday before she'd stumbled upon it, they'd found it within fifteen minutes.

Almost as though it wanted to be found.

"But come on. A wishing well?"

"I know it sounds crazy, but I did feel. . . I dunno, a strange chill when I was here before." She didn't tell him about the voice.

"A chill?" Still looking skeptical, he peered over the edge of the well. His expression shifted, as though deciding something. Then he dug around in his pockets and pulled out a penny.

"Bell, no." Desperation seeped into her voice. She lunged for the coin, but he held it up out of her reach, laughing.

"Only one way to know for sure, right?"

"I don't think that's a good idea." Her heart pounded in her ears. Was it just her or had the forest gone eerily silent?

"Here. I'll wish for something that would never happen.

That way, if it does, then we know for sure."

It *did* sound reasonable, and once he got something in his head, it was impossible to change his mind. There would be no dissuading him now.

She sighed. "Fine."

He closed his eyes and dropped the coin. No wind, no darkness.

"What did you wish for?"

His lips tipped up. "If I told you, it wouldn't come true."

"Pretty sure that's not how wishing wells work."

"Because you're an expert."

"Obviously." She smiled in spite of herself.

Bellamy checked his watch. "We better go. I promised Em I'd meet her."

"Right." River swallowed. For a second they had felt like the old Bell and River. But she had given that up when she'd kissed him, when she'd run away like a coward. Now they were both trapped in this excruciating limbo: not friends, not lovers—not even exes. At least exes would be a category she could have understood.

"You shouldn't blame yourself for the fire, you know," Bellamy said as they started back down the hill. "Wish or no wish."

But she *had* wished for it. Maybe that meant that deep down, she'd wanted it to happen.

At first, when the house phone rang in the middle of the night again, River thought she was caught in one of those time loops. But Bellamy's strangled voice on the other end yanked her into focus.

"It's Darryl. . . something happened."

Her heart leapt to her throat. So help her, if his step–dad had done something to him—

"He crashed his motorcycle," Bellamy continued.

River felt a wave of relief and then another one of guilt for being relieved that something so bad had happened. "Is everyone okay?"

"We don't know yet. He's in surgery. My mom. . . she's freaking out. . ."

"I'm coming right now."

"You don't have to—"

"Bell. I'm coming."

At the hospital, Bellamy's mom, Noreen, paced the waiting room aisle. Bellamy and Emily sat together, but they seemed strangely distant with each other.

Bellamy looked up as she walked in, his eyes hollow. "Riv?" Like he'd forgotten she was coming.

She gave Noreen a hug then took the seat on the other side of Bellamy.

"All these terrible things happening. . ." Emily said, ". . .even I'm starting to think there's something to all this stuff with the black dog."

"What do you mean?" River asked her.

"You didn't hear? The Murak brothers crashed their fishing boat and nearly caught hypothermia. And there's that slaughtered goat they found on the lake road near the camp."

Bellamy frowned. "Okay, that *is* weird."

"I didn't hear about that." River's throat tightened. This was worse than she thought. "Bell, can I talk to you real quick?" she asked, trying to disguise the shrill note of terror in her voice.

Emily gave them an odd expression, but watched Bellamy follow River to the hallway around the corner to where it was more private.

"What did you wish for?" she whispered.

He scrubbed his face and stared at her, confused. "What?"

"Your wish!" she hissed. "What was it for?"

"Not this!"

"Think carefully. What were your exact words?"

"I wished that—" He stopped, his expression going slack. "—that Darryl would go away." His Adam's apple bobbed, and horror darkened his eyes. "You don't think. . ."

River's insides felt like swirling serpents, and she thought she might be sick. She leaned against the icy, cinder block wall and rubbed her temples.

"I think I set something loose with my wish," she said hoarsely. "Something bad."

River felt eyes on her. The farther she walked into the bush, the more intense the feeling became. As though someone were right behind her. Twice she turned around, imagining a breath on the back of her neck. But there was nothing there.

She was supposed to meet up with Bellamy, but she'd gotten restless and started up the path on her own, planning on doubling back to meet him after a few minutes. But now that she thought of it. . . how long had it been?

River started walking back toward the trailhead. It had been years since this trail was properly maintained, but—probably mainly because of her and Bellamy wearing it down—you could still follow the faint path through the hills for several kilometers.

But just now, the trail looked unfamiliar. A cold stone grew in her gut. Had she really walked up this way only minutes ago? The path stretched out before her, ferns and fallen logs in all the wrong places, pleasant spots of shade turned into ominous shadows where anything could be lurking.

Footsteps in the thicket, slow and lumbering.

"Bell?" she called, her voice sharp against the gentle rustling language of the forest. River stopped near a towering White Pine. Maybe she had accidentally stepped off the path.

More footsteps. It was definitely too heavy to belong to a chipmunk or a field mouse. A black shadow shifted between two trees, then paused. It was huge, with black fur on a broad frame.

River froze. Bears weren't uncommon in this area. That's when she noticed the shape of the animal's snout, the thinness of its frame and long tail.

This wasn't a bear. Could it be a wolf?

Or the black dog, said a niggling voice in her head. Either way, she didn't want to get any closer to find out. Slowly, she backed away, mentally charting an escape route.

Something grabbed her shoulder.

River cried out and leapt away.

"Sorry, sorry! It's just me!" Bellamy held his hands in the air. "You didn't hear me calling your name?"

She shook her head, chest still quaking with adrenaline. When she glanced back to where she'd seen the dog, it was gone.

"Well, sorry. I didn't mean to scare you. Did you bring the coins?"

River fished a roll of pennies from her coat pocket and held it up.

Bellamy shook his head. "If this actually works, I'll be surprised."

The night of the motorcycle accident they'd gone to River's father for help. The three of them sat around the Meadows' kitchen table with mugs of strong black tea. But even a hot drink and the fire in the wood stove couldn't stave off the chill that seemed to linger in River's bones. They told him the whole story, well *almost*. River left out the part about what she'd wished for, a splinter of guilt inching its way into her heart.

"A wishing well, huh? Wishes are strong forces." Joe glanced between them. "Unspoken ones, perhaps even more so."

River chewed her lip as the splinter wormed even deeper. Bellamy aimlessly stirred his tea in silence.

Her father took a sip from his cup and swallowed. "Sounds like a bogle." River glanced at Bellamy who shrugged with a bewildered expression. "They like to make trouble," her dad continued. "Play tricks."

"Tricks?" River replied. Not exactly the word she would have used.

Her father continued, his face grim. "They cause accidents, play nasty pranks. Sometimes the outcome is. . . more severe."

"But. . . what is it?" she asked.

"Some say it's a ghost. Others say an imp or a demon that lives in the woods."

Bellamy scrubbed his face. Dark circles framed his eyes, and his brown curls, which were wild on a good day, flopped into his face in a frizzy mess. "How do we stop it?" he asked.

River's dad shook his head. "You can't stop it. It goes where it wants and does as it pleases. It's free."

"But it was imprisoned at some point, right?" she said. "It was in the well, and somehow I set it loose."

Bellamy straightened. "So there must be a way to trap it there again."

"In the stories they are attracted to shiny things," River's dad offered.

"The coins," River replied. "There were old coins jammed in between the stones of the well, into the trees." Hope gathered in her chest.

Bellamy set down his tea. "Maybe the coins were people's way of appeasing the bogle in the past?"

"Could that work?" River turned to her dad, the hope inside her sprouting wings. What if they could make this right?

"I don't know what we'll do if it doesn't."

In the woods, River and Bellamy dropped a trail of pennies on the path as they hiked toward the well. They walked mostly in an uncomfortable silence. River imagined the cries of the birds carrying all the words left unsaid between them.

At last they came upon the well, unremarkable in every way.

"How do we know if it's working?" Bellamy asked.

Before River could respond, a darkness fell over them, plunging the forest into shadow as dim as twilight.

A gust of wind kicked up a cloud of dead leaves, its chill sharper than the bite of winter.

"Come for another wish, little ones?" said the voice on the wind.

"What the. . ." Bellamy dropped the pennies in his hand, stricken.

"I can give you your wildest dreams," the bogle whispered in River's ear, using Bellamy's voice. "Exactly what you wish for." Now it was her dad's.

Bellamy, who had drifted to her side, opened his mouth to speak, but she shook her head. It couldn't find out what they were trying to do.

"Your wishes seem to have a cost," she said. They still couldn't see the creature. River scanned the trees, though she didn't know what she was looking for.

The shadows seemed to thicken above them. Darkness swirled together in the branches, hardening into head and limbs covered with reptilian skin. Bat-like wings with talons sprouted from its back. Its head resembled an illustration of a goblin River had seen in a storybook as a child: caricature-ish and horned with a wide, sharp-toothed grin. Only in real life it was infinitely more sinister. She had a feeling those teeth would have no problem tearing through flesh.

"Doesn't everything have a cost?" the bogle replied. It must have been its own voice because it rasped and creaked like rusty hinges. "Surely, there is something you want that's worth it."

Bellamy, who had grabbed her hand at some point, stepped forward, placing himself between River and the bogle.

"What do you have there?" This was directed at

Bellamy. River glanced down at the pennies in Bellamy's free hand. He must've retrieved the coins from when he dropped them earlier.

"These?" Bellamy released River's hand and inched toward the well. Slowly, he placed a few pennies onto the crumbling stone of the edge.

The bogle cocked its head. It was working!

Bellamy dropped the remainder of the coins into the well. The bogle spread its wings, which were bigger than they looked, and flapped them through the air. Then it lifted itself into the air and landed on the stone lip of the well. Bellamy leapt back, but the bogle didn't seem to notice him. Greedily, it scooped up the pennies and examined them. It put one between its teeth and bit down on it.

Please go down the well. Please go down the well. . . River thought desperately.

Almost as though it had heard her, the bogle looked up. It cocked its head again and grinned, showing teeth flecked with black and a reddish brown color that River tried to pretend didn't remind her of blood.

It tossed the pennies to the ground. "That wasn't a very good game. Too bad. Games are my favorite. I have a better idea." The bogle lifted off into the air, hovering just above their heads. "Maybe you can play with him."

Heavy footfalls tramped through the leaves behind them. River whirled around. Black fur on a broad frame.

It was the black dog, slowly materializing in the air before their eyes. Had the bogle been conjuring it this entire time?

"Oh no. . . " Bellamy breathed.

Up close it resembled a wolf more than a dog. Its eyes shone an unearthly yellow above impossibly long fangs.

"Please tell me you brought a weapon," River said under her breath, backing away from the creature.

"I brought my gun, but I left it in the truck." Bell's voice was threaded with tension.

"How is that helpful?"

He threw his hands in the air. "I don't know! I just thought I'd mention it!"

The black dog growled and stepped toward them. River and Bellamy inched backwards until the well stood between them and the black dog. But that wasn't going to do anything to stop it. She glanced around for the bogle, but it was gone.

"River! Bell!" a voice called through the trees.

Oh no. Before she could call out a warning, her father burst into the clearing. What was he doing here?

"Dad, watch out!" she called, but the dog was already lunging for him.

He tried to dodge, but it was too late. Her father was over six feet tall, but the beast knocked him down as though he were made of straw. He rolled away and scrambled to his feet, but not before the dog clamped down on his leg.

"Dad!" she shrieked, paralyzed. Suddenly Bellamy was

over there too, brandishing a fallen branch like a sword.

The dog released her dad and turned its attention on Bellamy.

River rushed over to help him up.

"What happened with the coins?" he gasped.

"Didn't work."

"You two get out of here," Bellamy called, not taking his eyes off the dog. Blood and drool foamed around its mouth.

"We're not leaving you here alone!" River shrieked, a sob clutching her throat.

"Take your dad to my truck and get my gun."

The dog snarled and snapped at the branch.

"That'll take way too long!" she protested. There had to be some other way of defeating the beast. After all, it wasn't a normal dog; it was a forest spirit. Magic.

Her gaze fell to the scattered pennies, gleaming like jewels in the underbrush. Why hadn't the coins worked? The bogle had once been imprisoned. That meant there was a way to do it again. But how? Maybe the two were connected.

Secrets are stronger than anything. . . Her dad's words came back to her. . . *even magic.*

No, this wouldn't work. This was crazy.

"Dad." She turned to him while he leaned on her for support. "I don't want to take over the store." She winced as the words rushed out. "And. . . it was me who wished it away."

Her dad stared at her for a long moment, probably

confused by the non sequitur, but then he nodded solemnly. "I know."

"You do?"

"What're you doing?" Bellamy yelled. "I told you to go!"

But her dad's expression shifted from confusion to one of comprehension. "Secrets. . ." he murmured.

". . . are stronger than anything," River finished.

"What?" Bellamy shouted. At that moment, the dog whimpered and recoiled in pain. Above them, a shriek pierced the air as a gray slip of a wing materialized.

"It's working!" River cried. "Secret wishes set it free, but if you say them out loud—" She broke off as Bellamy jumped backward as the beast lunged again. "Bell, tell a secret."

"Um okay. . ." He glanced over his shoulder at her. "I never really beat you at that race in third grade. I hid near the finish line and waited until you were close."

"I knew it!" River glanced up, but nothing had changed. "Maybe it has to be a bigger secret."

"Okay. . ." Bellamy paused then blurted out, "I broke up with Emily last week. I just didn't know how to tell you."

The bogle shrieked again, and now they could see part of its body. The dog wobbled on its feet as though disoriented.

"What? Why?"

River's dad nudged her. "Secrets."

"Right." Drops of sweat rolled down her spine. "I shouldn't have run away that night, and I've been thinking about it ever since." A flush warmed her neck and face, despite the chill.

The bogle was totally visible now, and it seemed to be straining against some unseen force.

"Me, too," Bellamy replied, his voice barely audible above the dog's snarls. It limped toward them, and now he easily kept it at bay with the branch.

The bogle swiped a claw at River. She ducked out of the way.

Bellamy tossed her the branch. Catching it awkwardly, she launched a blow at the bogle and missed. This wasn't working; she wasn't going to beat the creature with force.

"Bell. . . why did you break up with Emily?"

He looked back at her, his dark expression brightened by a tinge of hope in his eyes. "Because I don't love her. I. . ." He swallowed. "I love you. I think I always have."

"I love you, too." As River said the words, it was as though a colossal, sodden weight left her. But she barely had time to think about it because the bogle let out a great scream, so piercing it could have torn the trees in half. It flapped its wings in one last effort, but then it drifted over to the well, dissolving into shadow and then vanishing altogether.

"You won, little ones," it rasped out, "this time. . ."

At their feet, the dog faded first to a black mist, then into nothingness. Bellamy hunched over his knees, breathless.

River rushed to her father's side and helped him up.

"I'm so sorry, Dad." Tears welled up in her eyes. "If I had even an inkling that my wish would destroy the store... I only wished to not have to work there anymore—"

Still leaning on her for support, Joe grasped his daughter's other shoulder, filling her with warmth. "I know, sweetheart. I know."

Once the three of them had limped their way back to the trailhead and got Joe's leg treated by the hospital in Pembroke, it was the middle of the night. River and Bellamy helped him into bed. Then the two of them sat outside on the porch, waiting for the sun to leak over the edge of the horizon, talking about all the things they had left unsaid.

As for the well, they never found it again. Bellamy wanted to search for it, just to make sure the bogle was really gone, but River knew that some things were better left behind the safe sheen of a fairytale. Some secrets were meant to be spoken, but others should be kept by the forest, at the bottom of the well at the end of the world.

Sacrifice Rock

Effie Joe Stock

The wind twists from east to west and kisses my wispy cheeks with a familiar whisper. "She's coming." I turn to follow the calling—a familiar tug I know too well and have never bothered to resist.

An aching silence devours the air in place of crunching leaves as my feet pad across the autumn blanketed ground. It's been so long since they've crunched for me, so long since the forest snapped and crackled in response to my physical touch. A smile creeps across my face as a squirrel scurries from its tree to the ground, oblivious to my presence, its little paws making such a ruckus in the trees' last clothes of the year.

Knots in my stomach tighten in excitement, then flutter still as the calling grows stronger.

I wonder who she will bring to me this time?

A chill rushes past as the wispy form of a baby goat bounds in front of me, kicking its dainty little feet—hooves that never got the chance to carry the little goat through life, or jump on staggered rocks. Not a sound was heard by the living forest as the goat bleats and knickers, waiting only a moment for me to catch up.

My chuckles ring through the red, orange, and yellow cloaked trees like wind through a chime. I scoop the little goat into my arms, neither warmth nor the softness of its fur gracing my skin. It wouldn't feel me either. Strange how we could be so close to one another, and yet so far.

"Come, little one. Let us see who she brings to us today," I whisper, lips tickling its transparent ear.

We step out of the woods onto an old path which had been beaten too well into the forest floor for it to give in to the wild just yet, and I catch sight of the girl whose weeping had called my soul to hers.

"Here she is. See who she has brought you," the wind whispers to me again.

I follow the girl until she reaches the small bluff that overlooks the dark expanse of the forest. With shaking legs, she kneels to the dirt, unaware that her nice jeans will now be stained from the moist, decomposing leaves.

If I still had a physical heart, it would have lurched in my chest as I watch her.

Gently, as if the poor animal can still feel something, she lowers the unmoving body of a white and black cat to the large, flat, empty rock.

"Sacrifice rock," I whisper, repeating the name this girl had given the rock the first time she had brought to my forest the still form of an animal she had once loved.

The little goat squirms out of my arms as I kneel in front of the girl. He bounds to her side and prances around her, nibbling on her clothes, and nuzzling her cheek. She doesn't know he is here; she doesn't know that she isn't alone. Yet, as if it were yesterday, I remember her whispering his name for the last time when she had brought his small, motionless body to sacrifice rock.

"Tango," I whisper it again as he lays by her side.

Placing my hand on the cat's soft fur, I wait to hear what she calls it.

For a long time, all the forest echoes back are the girl's quiet sobs. She tries to wipe the tears from her eyes, tries to smother the pain her heart is crying out. No matter how much she tries, she won't be able to stop this ache in her chest—love with nowhere else to go now that the creature she loved has died.

I move close and wrap my arms around her. She cannot see me, nor can she feel me, just as she is unaware of Tango at her other side, bleating at her and nibbling the distress in her jeans. But I wish to believe that somehow her heart is comforted by my promise to watch over this creature she has loved.

"It's all right, sweet girl. It's all right to cry. It's all right to love. It's all right to. . . let go."

She takes a shaking breath, presses her lips to the cat's soft fur, brushes her fingers across the little pale nose as if the cat is only sleeping, and whispers her name to the wind—letting it carry the word into the forest. "Stardust."

I've not cried a single tear since the day I woke up in the forest, an unseen, unheard, and forgotten shepherd of lost things. But even still, my heart aches alongside hers with the all too familiar pain of losing something you can never get back.

When she whispers the rest of the words she needs to say the most, a new emotion takes root in her grieving soul—relief.

"Goodbye, Stardust."

I kiss the girl's forehead just before she stands. "I promise I'll take good care of her," I whisper.

Then, as she says a prayer to the God she is devoted to, thanking Him for the little life she had loved for not nearly long enough, I press my lips to the cat's ear and whisper the words the forest once whispered to me so many years ago.

"*Wake up.*"

Wispy eyes blink open; the cat slowly takes to her feet, stretches and yawns, leaving her physical body behind, and joining me in this quiet sanctuary in the forest.

"Say goodbye, Stardust." I gently push the cat toward

the girl hugging herself and wrestling with her grief.

As the girl turns to walk away, the cat meows and purrs, rubbing herself against her legs. She is pleading for one last pet, one last touch, one last kiss that I know will never come.

The leaves crunching under her feet, the girl trudges back up the hill, disappearing down the road from which she came.

"Goodbye for now, sweet girl," I whisper, though I know she will never hear me. "I will see you again." I smile sadly as Tango and Stardust stop following the girl. Ceasing their pitiful cries for her to return to them. They finally turn back toward me.

Though I don't know what drove her to bring the first beloved animal to sacrifice rock only a few years ago, I believe the forest brought us together, knowing my lonely heart needed her the same way her grief needed me. I know this well. Though her heart may resent death, never forgetting little Stardust, her soul has found some peace. Deep down she knows I am here taking care of all the little creatures she has brought me and the forest to care for.

Picking up Tango and calling for Stardust to follow, I slowly drift back into the woods, letting the wind push me back into autumn spotted branches where tens of other passed on animals wait for me. Lambs, goats, chickens, ducks, and dogs—each a creature she had raised and loved, and then, in the stillness of their death, had brought back to the forest, to where they will live on eternally under my watch, safe in the arms of the trees, knowing no pain, or fear, or sorrow.

And one day, the girl's heart will heal. She will learn to love again. Then, when it is time for another creature to pass on, she will bring their precious form to the forest and I will meet her. To take into my arms whoever else she brings to me at sacrifice rock.

Death Lies in the Wych Elm

Anayis Der Hakopian

Every town and river
    Has its calls and curves
    Fables and whispers
They carry in their waters
Freezing in the winter
Reawaken in the spring
And shows the bodies rotting
In the boiling summer feat
The lores return well
In the days of ember fall
To remind us to be fearful
And especially wary
Of what we believe we know
We joke of such stories
To get rid of the shivers
For the hint of curses are damning

But here in Hagley
There is in fact a true curse
A tale carved into bark
That calls for its prey:
"In the woods beyond the hall
Pass those river bends
Where the elm trees stand
With something hollow in one's hand
They are witching with their branches
Stretching in all their grabbing dances
For here the roots of the underworld lay
The core sipping black into the land
With singed long clawed fingered hands
Slipping through the earth's broken cracks
Curling around those with a darkened hold
On the ones who least expect it to show."
For there was a woman who stood astray
Who did not know the curse that lay in wait
In those woods that she would cross through
Something was pulling at the roots
Sending a cry out into the broken veil
For death was hiding in those trees
Waiting for Bella to wander near
For the elm to swallow her whole—here
She was held stuck in a binding cage
And shaken till there was no breath

The House Built Between the Branches

Flesh rotted, bone remaining
She stayed waiting for someone to come calling
To find her soul lost in the wych elm's hold
To cut her from the nails of the underworld's woes
And let her rest in the stay of earthly home
But poor Bella had no one to call
She was found by chance
In a time long past
Left unrested in the braided hand
Stirring spilling stillness strands
Cursebled, unspoken and broken
Much like the words of trusted men
Who were happy to lay whispers to rest
So death itself kept drifting
Within the elm tree's branches
And was never caught red handed
But it still lurked in the wood's shadows
In the living and dead—it had done it
It became a lure, a curse, a fearful story
For the people continue asking in her stead
Who put Bella in the wych elm tree?

Demons and Dekkonali

Hannah Carter

"I told you this was a bad idea." Ellaesandra—or, Elly, as her friends called her—crept past the line of barren oak trees. A branch cracked under her foot. Shivering, she held out her hand and willed a tiny ball of light, courtesy of a lux spell, to appear.

"Would you quit saying that? You're such a downer. This is why we don't get invited to parties." A few steps ahead of Elly, Massie slipped under the dead branches of the canopy without so much as a sound. Even with the light spell, Elly had to squint to see her friend, swathed in all black, even up to her headscarf. But as soundless as Massie's feet were, her mouth made up the difference.

"I thought we didn't get invited to parties because we're both introverts." Elly wished she would have grabbed a coat back when Massie picked her up. Now, she could only rub her cold, goosefleshed arm and curse her past self.

Massie turned around, a mischievous glint in her dark eyes. "I mean, yeah, that's probably about ninety percent of the reason, but the other ten percent is because you're such a killjoy." Her alto voice carried a hint of a smile, along with an accent, like all her spoken words were slightly cursive.

Elly rolled her eyes. With a few strides, she caught up to Massie and slugged her friend's arm. But all Elly's joviality disappeared as a barn owl hooted. A shiver slid down her spine, and she edged closer to Massie. "I really don't think we should have come alone. Can we turn around now before we end up murdered?"

"No one's going to murder us." Massie tilted her head up to glare at Elly. The tilt was necessary—with her natural elven height, Elly towered over Massie. But even at eighteen, Massie barely stood at four-feet-eight-inches. Elly more than likely would have towered over her friend even without the genetic advantage of being an elf. "Not if you stick with me, kid."

Elly rolled her eyes. "I'm worried that's exactly why they'll murder me."

Massie chuckled and crept further back. "Ready to explore a supposedly demon-infested cabin in the woods?"

"No. I'm not. Do you know why? Because it's a '*cabin in the woods.*'" Elly curled her palm in and whispered "*desinmere*" to the tiny ball of light to extinguish it. The candle that illuminated the window of a small, rundown cabin suddenly became much more interesting. "I think the three best adjectives to describe it are spooky, dilapidated, and eerie."

Massie hummed in the back of her throat. "Are you sure spooky and eerie aren't synonyms?"

Elly quirked an eyebrow, her voice monotone. "Does it matter?"

"Actually, it does. Because if you can replace spooky with eerie, then you need another adjective."

Elly grunted. "Fine." She rolled through a few more suggestions in her head as they crept closer. In the glow of the candlelight, she thought she could see a human-sized shadow flicker. Maybe that was just in her head? "Does haunted count as a synonym of spooky or eerie?"

Massie cocked her head. "The jury is still out."

A bird cawed from overhead as they approached the steps. Elly sucked in a breath, her teeth clenched. A chilly breeze rattled the branches and carried a scent of autumn: death, decaying leaves, a tinge of smoke from some distant fire pit. . . and a bit of fear.

Elly grabbed for Massie's shoulder, bunching up the fabric there to draw Massie closer. There was no way Elly was ready. But if she gave into her trepidation now, she'd be worse than a coward, so she didn't protest any more as they reached the derelict cabin.

Massie put her foot on the first step. The forest seemed

to go quiet. Elly flinched as the second stair let out a long creak. With each successive step, the noise announced their presence to the whole woods.

The blasted barn owl hooted again and caught Elly off guard. She whirled around, hand already extended to throw a spell at anyone behind them.

Nothing but the large, dead trees stared back at her. A cloud drifted in front of the moon and cast odd shadows on the ground, like wriggling demons come to steal the girls' souls.

"Are you sure we can do this alone?" Elly whispered. Her voice cracked, and even that soft murmur sounded too loud. "I know it's important, but—"

"There's no *but*. If we're going to exorcize this demon, it has to be done tonight. You're free to back out if you're too scared, though." Massie grasped the doorknob in her hand. "But if I turn this door, you're coming in and we're doing this together."

Elly swallowed. "My parents will be so mad if we get murdered. My dad will probably resurrect our corpses just so he can ground us both, then kill us again." She tried to pitch her voice up at the end to make the joke land, but nerves made her voice shake regardless.

"Sounds like a fun time." Massie held up three fingers with her other hand. "You have until the count of three to back down. One." A twig snapped. "Two."

Elly's heartbeat whooshed inside her ears. She licked her lips.

"Three." Massie wiggled her fingers. "All right. You're in."

"Yeah. I can't let you do this alone." Elly shivered in the bitter air as it blew dead leaves around. They rattled like bones in the wind—had the temperature dropped since the beginning of the countdown?

Massie pressed those three fingers to her lips in a "shush" gesture. She opened the door, her eyes still locked on Elly's.

The floorboards creaked underneath their feet as the girls crossed the threshold. Two shattered windows bookended both sides of the cabin. A single candle flickered on a table on the right side of the room—the light Elly had seen from afar. A rocking chair, missing a few pieces of wood in its back, seemed to rock by itself—or maybe Elly's nerves made her imagine that.

A large shadow loomed beside the door.

Elly shrieked, all silence forgotten. She held up her hand and yelled, "*ignis*"—the fire spell was the first one that popped into her mind. "Die, demon!" She hurled a fireball at the man-sized shadow.

Massie yipped and wrenched free of Elly's grip. She dove for the figure, dagger extended. She drove it into the shadow man several times, careful to avoid the flames, until—

Massie broke off into a bit of nervous laughter. "No demon whatsoever. Just a now-maimed coat stand."

"Huh?" Elly held out her hand. "*Desinmere*." She snuffed out the remaining flames swallowing her hands and started a *lux* spell to fill the room with more light than the candle could offer. She knelt next to Massie and touched the now burned and hole-ridden men's coat. ". . .Oh."

Massie sighed. "So much for being quiet." She sheathed her dagger and wiggled her fingers in Elly's direction. "Someone's a touch jumpy, though, aren't they?"

Elly rolled her eyes. "Shut up. Unlike you, I'm new to all this stuff."

Massie traced the new tattoos on her face—a red line that went from her lips to the bottom of her chin, straight through the tiny dimple there. Three white circles rested on either side of her cheeks. "Just consider it a little adventure. And. . ." Massie's voice sounded surprisingly sentimental as she added, "I'm glad you're here on this adventure with me, Elly."

Elly grunted. "Yeah, yeah. I guess if I'm going to get murdered, I'd rather be murdered with you."

"That's what best friends are for, right?" Massie rose to her feet. "That, and killing coats. Best friends have very versatile uses."

Elly snorted. "And to borrow hair ties when you forget them."

"Okay, but that's a necessity." Massie felt her wrist. "Speaking of which, I didn't bring one. But I don't need one right now, anyway."

"You better not. I didn't include it on my '*late-night excursions to demon-infested cabins in the woods*' packing list," Elly replied dryly. She hadn't included a coat, either. Or anything else.

"Well, that's an oversight on your part."

The two turned their attention back to the main room. There was a door behind the broken rocking chair, standing half-open. Another one, closed tightly, rested near the candle Elly had spied from outside. Aside from the furniture Elly had already seen, the only other things in the room were leaves that had skittered in when the door had opened.

Elly put her hands against the wall and trailed around the room. Behind her, a knock sounded every once in a while as Massie paced around the opposite wall.

"You hear that?" Massie asked.

Elly froze, her hands near the broken window. She strained her ears in the silence. "Hear what?"

Massie tilted her head. If she'd been a dog right then, Ellie might have sworn her friend's ear would have actually twitched. "Crying. I think."

Ellie swallowed, her throat suddenly dry. "Then we're on the right track." A few more steps and she reached the door behind the rocking chair. She willed the light ball in her hand to glow a little bit brighter as she threw it open and—

Stairs crawled up toward oblivion.

"Oh, goodie. I've always wanted to go into the attic of a supposedly haunted house."

Massie came up behind her. "Sorry about your luck, but we're not going to the attic. I don't hear crying coming from up there." She shifted her weight a few times, cocking her head at different angles like a curious pup. They both paused when a loud *creak* filled the air. "But as a consolation prize, how do you feel about a haunted *basement*?"

Elly turned around, mouth open, but nerves stilled her tongue. She could find no quick joke to cover her anxiety now.

Massie took a few steps back, paused, and then moved the broken rocking chair over a few feet. She bent down, hand tapping around the worn floor, only to let out a tiny exclamation. "Look." Massie grunted as she pried open a trap door, which groaned loudly.

"Shh!" Elly hissed.

Massie rolled her eyes. "You're shushing the floor, silly."

Elly cleared her throat as she rubbed her arms.

Massie chuckled as she reached for the candle. "Hey. Any clue why a demon would need a light?"

"Maybe the fire reminds him of home?"

Massie snorted, leaning down to examine the hole. Elly crept over so she could peer over Massie's shoulder. A ladder led down into. . . something?

"Who goes first? Draw straws?" Massie whispered.

"No. It's only logical that I go first." Elly's voice cracked.

Despite the fear, she forced herself closer to the ladder. "Put that candle down before you burn something." She turned her attention back to the orb in her outstretched palm. But this time, instead of merely making it shine brighter, she decided to put one of her Advanced Spellcasting classes to use. "*Sursumanete.*" She focused her magic on the ball. A bead of sweat rolled down her cheek. "*Sursuvivina. Sursumanete. Sursuvivina.*" With each incantation, the light floated higher and thrummed with power. When it hovered near her shoulder Elly gripped the ladder and began the descent. The loyal little lux spell bobbed alongside her.

The railing groaned in her white-knuckle grip. The air tasted stale this far down, tainted with old water and other unmentionable smells. If Elly hadn't clenched her jaw so tightly, she might have thrown up.

This is a demon's den. What did you expect? A field of flowers? Perhaps a tea shop?

Her feet hit the floor. The climb had been twelve feet, maybe a little more—but it had felt so much worse.

With one more putrid inhale, Elly turned around and faced the demon's inner sanctum.

It felt even colder down in these depths, and Elly once again cursed her past self's decision to not bring a coat. What had she been thinking by not grabbing one? Well—she hadn't been thinking. There tended to be an abundance of *not thinking* when she and Massie plotted together.

Feet *thudded* on the floor beside her. Elly bit off a swear and swallowed. Massie grinned in response. The glow from the lux ball cast eerie shadows on her tattooed face—almost as if she should be the one feared in this unexplored world.

"You're terrifying," Elly whispered.

"Thanks." Massie patted Elly's shoulder and took the lead. "I try."

They crept down a long, cobblestone hallway. Cries echoed around them, louder than they had been up top, amplified by the stony walls. Elly hunched over, though for once, she didn't need to, since her head didn't brush the top of the ceiling. How considerate of the demons that built this creepy cabin in the woods to think about elven height.

Someone wailed in the distance.

"That sounded pretty demonic to me," Elly said. She reached for Massie's sleeve again.

"I know, right? Exciting." Massie's voice carried a bit of a sarcastic bite. "Remember, no backing out."

"I know." Elly sighed and leaned in close. "But there's still time to go get your par—"

"Absolutely not." Massie rested a hand against her dagger and growled—a wolfish and guttural sound, and Elly once again got the distinct image of her friend as a dog, hair all on end. "My parents can't come. You've known that all along. If you didn't want to do this, you should have left when I gave you until the count of three."

"No. I do want to help. It's just. . ." Elly's eyes roamed the dark corridor. She rubbed her chest like she could assuage the hurt there which intensified with every not-too-distant sob. How could she put it into words—the feeling of being terrified while doing the right thing? "Everything feels wrong. I'm just. . . scared."

"Yeah." Massie turned the corner first and stopped. Her shoulders went rigid, and her fingers curled against the hilt of her weapon. "But they are, too."

Elly followed her around the bend and sucked in a breath. Her eyes widened, filling with tears.

Everywhere. There were children everywhere.

Children chained to walls. Children stuffed in cages. Some of them shied away from the light as it floated by or hid their faces. Others had no reaction whatsoever, their faces despondent masks. A few adjusted their positions, their chains clinking and groaning against each other.

"Who are you?" a boy asked. Elly guessed he was maybe eleven or twelve. "Are you gonna buy us?"

Elly's voice congealed in her throat, like she might choke on it. Every time she swallowed, the lump seemed even bigger.

Somehow, Massie managed to speak, but her voice still sounded gruff. She seemed to walk a bit more hunched over than she usually did, too. "We're not buyers."

Another little child sniffed. "You're not here for our blood?"

A few of them wailed or called for their parents. Elly moved closer to a little girl; the poor thing flinched before Elly had even knelt down beside her. Elly swallowed. Her heart yearned to reach for the toddler and hold her as close as the chains would allow. Yet Elly held back, for fear of scaring the child worse.

The toddler looked like she had endured unspeakable horrors. Her dark skin could barely conceal the outline of her bones. And the smell was so much worse up close—Elly knew she couldn't cover her nose. These children weren't responsible for the horrid fumes, but she still had to choke down a gag. She wouldn't let them see her react. She wouldn't let them think she felt disgusted by them when really, all her disgust was aimed at the situation.

Elly patted the girl's head. "No, we're not. I promise. We're here to get you out."

"How?" one of the bigger ones bleated. "You don't understand. The—the bad man in the house. He owns our blood."

Elly swallowed. She glanced over at Massie, but her best friend didn't meet her gaze. Instead, Massie sat, hunched over, hands on either side of her head.

Had even Massie reached the limit of what she could take?

No. They had to pull themselves together. They were older, more prepared. . .

Elly choked back a sob. That was such a lie. She wasn't

prepared for this. No one, not even Massie or her parents, could *ever* be prepared for the amount of misery here. To witness these atrocities up close.

The child had been wrong about one thing: there was no man in the house. There was, truly, only a demon masquerading in human skin.

But he wouldn't win today. "No one is going to take anyone's blood." Elly bent down and deposited the child back among her peers.

"You don't have to worry," Massie rasped. "Have any of you heard about the Dekkonali?"

The children all answered in the negative through either words or shakes of their heads.

Massie took a deep breath. "The Dekkonali are a clan of werewolves who vowed long ago to protect those that were being persecuted. With the Composer's blessing, we pledged to free the innocent from the grasp of evil, wherever it may be." Massie raised up to her full height and turned around. Her eyes glowed golden as they locked on Elly's. "That is my pledge, as a loyal Daughter of the Dekkonali. Tonight, I am going to get you out of here, and strike down the demon holding you hostage."

Elly took a few steps forward and grasped her best friend's hand. She interlocked their fingers and nodded. Her heart skittered while her brain raced with a million ways this mission could go wrong. But this was Massie's sacred duty, no matter how dangerous and terrifying it seemed to Elly.

"Me, too," Elly murmured. She may not have been a Daughter of the Dekkonali, but she was a best friend. Freeing hostages and loaning hair ties—all included in the best friendship package.

Massie grinned, and a few fangs poked over her lips as she wavered on the precipice of a full transformation. "And there's no one I'd rather explore a creepy cabin in the woods with. Even if it is spooky and eerie."

"And demon-infested." Elly shuddered, but that could have been the chill in the air or the stench that invaded her nose. "Don't forget demon-infested."

"Speaking of a demon. . ." Massie glanced around. "Maybe we better get these kids out while he's not here. Set me up a portal?"

"Always." Elly turned toward a free spot in the center of the room. She hadn't yet officially graduated yet, but she'd applied for a portaling license early when Massie had received her latest orders. Only an elf could open a portal, and lucky for everyone, Elly would very much risk her life for Massie and a good cause.

After all, the true measure of friendship was whether or not you'd kill for someone.

"*Portarius*." Elly moved her hand in a circle and watched the first sparks of magic appear. The sparkles of blue, purple, and pink twisted together in midair, growing larger as she conducted this silent orchestra.

Metal crashed behind her. Elly flinched; the magic sputtered. She whipped around and saw Massie, now in her werewolf form, with the chains of a child in her teeth. She wrenched and yanked at the iron, but it refused to break.

Massie leaned back onto her haunches and turned human again, the transformation instantaneous. "*Ahckrit.*"

Elly snickered at the Atlantean curse word. "Tsk, tsk. Language."

Massie grinned, though it didn't reach her eyes. "It doesn't count as cursing if you say it in a different language." She paused. "Just. . . don't tell my mother."

Elly made an *x* over her heart. "On my honor."

Massie knelt down and attempted to pick the lock with her dagger. Elly returned to her portal.

The minutes trickled by. Every noise made Elly glance to the hall where they'd entered. They were almost done. This was the last step. Massie's father had tracked the demon and learned his patterns for months leading up to this initiation. Preferably, they needed to get the children out of the basement before he returned from his weekly black market trip. But if Massie couldn't get the shackles undone. . .

"Done," Massie whispered. A quiet *clang* broke the terse atmosphere—she must have put the shackle on the ground. "One down."

Elly stared at her half-finished portal. A bead of sweat trailed down her spine and made her uncomfortable. "Great. You've got one kid half undone. If you wouldn't mind hurrying. . ."

"Have *you* ever tried lockpicking something by yourself in a high-stakes environment? It's not easy, and I've been trained for it since I was ten." Massie ran her arm over her own sweaty forehead. "Have some patience."

"I'll *have patience*, but I highly doubt our demon friend will if he gets here. Especially if he brings. . ." Elly's voice trailed off. She cleared her throat, and switched the word buyers to: ". . . friends."

A few children whimpered or whined. They clawed at their bonds, rattled the bars of the cages, and jerked against the wall.

"Don't let him take us!" one cried.

"Shh, shh. Nobody's taking anyone anywhere. Well—I suppose that isn't true. We're taking you to the Dekkonali safe house." Elly wiped her sweaty palms one at a time against her shirt. The entire mission hinged on this. "On the other side of this portal, you'll find some nice clan members who will protect you—Massie's parents." Elly nodded to her friend, who had gone to work on the second shackle on the first child.

"All right. You're free." Massie crossed to the next child—the little girl Elly had knelt beside earlier.

The first freed boy scampered over, his dark eyes wide. "Can I go through?"

Elly glanced at the swirling magic. All the threads had combined and seemed to hold steady. She could do this. Nothing would go wrong. The mission was almost over. "Yes. And once you go through, just pop back over and let me know you see Massie's parents and you're safe."

The boy nodded.

Elly closed her eyes and prayed as she felt him jump through. The magic fluctuated but never gave out.

Seconds ticked by. Her anxious mind checked and rechecked the weave of her spell. This was a basic portal. She hadn't sent him far, and she certainly hadn't sent him to another world. The moon conditions weren't ideal for that, nor were they conducive to time travel, so there was no way she had abandoned him in some distant future or past. She'd done her part perfectly. He would be safe. Soon *all* the kids would be safe.

Another bead of sweat trailed down Elly's skin.

The boy popped back in through the portal, his face aglow. "It worked! I see them! I mean—I saw them!"

"Oh, thank goodness." Elly breathed a sigh of relief.

Scrawny arms circled her. "Thank you." The boy scurried off to Massie, who'd almost freed yet another child, this one imprisoned behind bars. "Thank you both."

Massie smiled. "If you really want to thank us, move

your tail. Jump through that portal and leave this nightmare behind you."

The boy nodded. "And. . . good luck. Facing the bad man, I mean."

"Thanks." Massie grunted as she freed the small girl. "Here. Take her, too."

The two children latched hands and sprinted through the portal.

Elly held it firm as it rippled. Two down, twelve left to go.

From down the long hallway, she heard the loud squeal of the trap door opening.

The children shrieked. Massie swore again in Atlantean. Elly screamed, and the portal rippled.

Footsteps approached. Shadows shifted.

"Hurry, hurry," Massie muttered. She jerked on another chain, but it didn't give.

A pale man with bright blonde hair stalked into the room, hands behind his back. He wore a brown vest over a rumpled white button-up shirt. He looked like a frumpled professor—not anything like a demon. But Elly knew what he was.

Looks could be so deceiving—especially where vampires were concerned.

"Now, what do we have here?" The professor slowly turned from one girl to the other. "Someone trying to steal my wares?"

"These are children," Massie spat. "Not your things to

buy and sell as you please."

"Oh, on the contrary." The professor fiddled with the top button on his shirt. It unbuttoned, revealing a sliver of pale chest underneath. "You can buy and sell anything in this world. The only thing is how legal it seems to the rest of the world."

Massie spread her feet in a protective stance, her dagger leveled at the man's heart.

The professor's red eyes dragged over to Elly. He sniffed. "Ah—an elf? Have you ever thought of selling yourself? Elf blood is a rare treat to vampires. So rare and exotic, what with how elves prefer single-child families. You could be a blood bank. Or blood slave, if you'd prefer to only be bitten by one person."

Elly's nostrils flared. "I'd prefer not to be bitten by anyone."

The professor shrugged. "Did you think I was offering you a choice in the matter?" He flashed a smile, protruded fangs on full display, and lunged straight for Elly.

She screamed as his fingers dug into her neck. Her portal flickered out of existence as the two of them tumbled to the floor. Elly's head smacked against the stone. Stars blurred her vision, and everything throbbed.

She couldn't think quickly enough. Couldn't get her tongue to articulate a spell. The vampire plunged toward her neck, fangs extended—

Massie in wolf form collided with his side. Blood

splattered against the floor as Massie dug her teeth into the man's side. He snarled, venom dripping from his teeth.

"Mutt!" He swiped his claws at Massie's snout. The blow broke skin and left three jagged scratches. Blood mingled with fur and stained her teeth as the professor shoved her off. A bit of fabric from his vest tore away, which gave him an even shabbier appearance.

He shoved his long, wavy bangs away from his glowing red eyes. "Insolent mutt."

Elly gripped his ankle and wheezed, "*Ignis!*"

Fire sputtered to life on his pant leg.

The professor roared, and the children cried out in suit. He kicked toward Elly's face with his fiery leg; she jerked out of the way so she wouldn't be burned, though the heat grazed her.

Massie snarled and pounced again. The professor caught her this time and drove his fangs into her neck while she howled. Her back legs pedaled in mid-air, and her front claws scratched at nothing. The professor tossed her to the ground, spat, and dragged his arm across his mouth, leaving a smear of Massie's blood behind.

"Pity only non-magical beings can be turned, but that poison should slow your friend down." He swatted at the fire on his legs until he extinguished it.

Massie staggered and collapsed on the floor.

The professor's eyes sparked. "I'd love to taste your rare blood, though, little elf-girl." He lunged for Elly's neck.

Elly thrust her arm out in front of her to intercept the blow. He buried his teeth in her forearm instead, and she screamed as teeth met bone. Her head already swirled from hitting it earlier, but with each second he clung to her, she could practically feel his venom poisoning her bloodstream. Her arm trembled, her mind foggy.

She raised up her free hand and shoved at his face. "*Ignis!*"

He shrieked, caught in the blaze. Elly's mind had stopped registering the smell of filth somewhere along the way, but she gagged once more at the stench of flesh and scorched hair.

The professor roared. Blood splashed across Elly's face and neck, and he jerked away, tearing bits of her flesh as he did.

Pain radiated through every inch of her.

He gripped her wrist and twisted it until it snapped. Elly's vision faded to black for a moment before she came to with a wail. Pain. Fire. Blood.

She kicked at his groin with whatever few moments of strength she had left and missed. Her spell died, unable to continue as Elly fought for consciousness. The professor hovered over her, smirking. The only remnants of her fire attack were singed hair and burns in the shape of her palm on the right side of his face.

The professor snarled, poised for an attack.

Until he coughed, soaking Elly in crimson once more.

Above him, Massie withdrew her dagger from his back

and stabbed him again. Once, twice—Elly lost count as Massie attacked the demon until he released his chokehold and slumped over.

Dead.

Massie left her weapon lodged in his heart and crawled over and gathered Elly's head into her lap and smoothed back the corkscrew curls plastered to Elly's forehead. Massie quivered as her eyes ran over Elly's frame.

"Thank you," Massie murmured. "It's all over. It's all over. I'll take care of you." She leaned her head against the wall. Blood trickled down from the three scratches across her nose, and her own eyes seemed hazy. "I've got you, Elly."

Elly smiled as she slipped into unconsciousness.

"You so owe me. Whatever privileges you get for becoming an official Daughter of the Dekkonali, I want them." Elly sat in Massie's house, along with the fourteen children they'd rescued. Though the venom had left Massie groggy, she'd managed to free the rest of the children and get back to the safe house and her parents. She'd also dragged Elly's unconscious body back, too, where Elly had received the proper fussing and nurturing. Even her broken wrist had been set in preparation for her father to heal it when she got home.

The injury still hurt, but as Elly watched fourteen famished faces feast on Massie's mother's food the next day, it all seemed worth it.

"The Dekkonali only get the pride of knowing they helped someone," Massie's father said, his voice a deep bass. He brought some more rolls to the table.

Massie snickered. "Yeah. So congratulations on your pride, and the knowledge that you now must dedicate your life to righting wrongs everywhere, no matter the cost to your own life."

Elly's gaze swept around the room. "Seems like a fair trade off. I get why you enjoy this whole Daughter of the Dekkonali thing."

Massie waited until her parents drifted back into the kitchen before she spoke again. "Thank you. Really." She reached for Elly's hand. "I know it was scary, but think of all that we did. You and I rescued these kids, and at the same time, more Dekkonali were raiding other trafficking rings. Mum said we saved almost *fifty* victims last night. Pretty good for your first mission, huh?"

A few tears slipped down Elly's cheeks, her smile so wide that she tasted her salty tears before she could wipe them away. "Yeah. A pretty good first mission." Even if she did wish that *some* of last night's memories would be buried by the sands of time. She only wanted to remember the happy children as they laughed and smiled at each other.

Massie squeezed Elly's hand again. "I'm glad to have such a brave best friend like you."

"And I'm glad to have a fierce best friend like you." Elly leaned against Massie's shoulder.

"You know, even if you weren't born into the clan, I think I can safely say. . . you're a true Daughter of the Dekkonali. A protector of innocents." Massie snuggled closer, and warmth swelled within Elly's heart. "And the truest of friends."

The Roe Girl

Vanessa E. Howard

The Carters Guild was daft to think its members would pay a toll to go through this forest, even if it did cut two hours from their trip. Alek shrugged and pulled the measuring string from his sack. As long as they paid him for mapping the shortcut, they could be as raving mad as they liked. He looped the string in his hands, eyeing the darkness between the towering trees, and stepped off the safety of the roadway bordering the woods.

Tying the string to a sapling at the edge of the trees, he began his work, determined not to jump at every little leaf rustle. The dimness beneath the treetops gave him a sense of entering a different realm.

The Forest of Adelade was a no man's land. It belonged to the creatures of story. Tales told around the fire to wide-eyed children. Ghost stories swapped over a mug of brew. Legends shared about mysterious maidens and hungry monsters.

The House Built Between the Branches

Years ago, as a lanky boy with an energetic imagination, he had soaked in the stories, wishing they were true, itching to meet a wood sprite or a forest imp. But manhood had replaced that dreaminess with practicality. Now, he believed in numbers, measurements, and facts. And the numbers told him he needed this job to pay for his credentials as a mapmaker. Credentials meant bigger jobs and more money. The childhood wish to meet a legendary creature became a sensible wish to get out of these woods alive and collect his fee.

Alek got out his journal and lead stylus, sketching a rough drawing of the area and marking where the trees stood. Spreading, sprawling giants that were rumored to be several hundred years old. They would all need to be cut down. He stretched the string and counted the knots, recording the measurements in his journal.

Something moved off to his left, but when he jerked his head around, there was nothing. A bird shrieked in the distance. A distinct sensation of being watched made him shiver all the way to his boots. Retrieving his string, he re-tied it and measured it again. Sketch, count, measure, record. Deeper into the wood. Deeper into the shadows. Deeper into this fabled place.

Each step intensified his nervousness. A squirrel chittering from a branch made him drop his stylus and a lizard scuttling past his feet prompted a near-squeal, which he quickly turned into a manly grunt. From the corner of his eye, he caught a glimpse of antlers. But then they were gone. He kept working, watching the edges of his vision more carefully. There it was. A quick blur. Antlers, a flash of tawny hide, a face.

A *face*?

Alek hurried in that direction. *There*! Delicate antlers and tangled hair. Then gone. Twigs cracked. Leaves swished. Branches swayed. Whatever it was, it didn't want to be followed. He tried to pick up his pace, but the forest seemed to work against him. Gnarled roots tripped him. Thorns snagged his breeches. He pushed one branch out of the way and he could have sworn it pushed back.

He stopped. The toll road wouldn't go this direction and why on earth was he following some mystery creature into the dark woods? Turning on his heel, he headed back to his original route. Get the map done. Get paid. Get his credentials.

A throaty growl sounded above him. He froze.

Slinking along a limb was a feline body with viciously sharp teeth protruding from its upper jaw and four-inch claws on each paw. Its tail wrapped tight around the branch and it, too, ended in claws. A treecat. He'd heard stories of the agile creatures that could kill with a single swipe of paw or tail. Reports of people surviving a treecat were nearly unheard of.

The growl rumbled again. Alek took a slow step back. The treecat padded forward. Its tail unwound from the branch and swished, claws slicing through the air.

Alek wore a small knife, more for utility than protection. His hand crept toward the hilt. The cat's haunches shifted into a jumping stance. He got his fingertips on the knife just as the cat sprang.

Burning pain sliced across his right shoulder and arm. The weight of the cat never hit.

A roe deer hurtled past him, antlers lowered, and plowed into the treecat. The cat rolled and came up snarling. Claws swept through the air as the creature gave a vicious swipe. Spinning on its front feet, the roe kicked out with its powerful hind legs. Its hooves caught the cat a glancing blow across its head. The deer struck again but missed. Hissing and growling, the cat backed away. Another wicked kick came from the roe, connecting with the feline's leg as it tried another swipe. That was enough for the treecat. It snarled one final time and disappeared into the brush.

Alek stumbled. The burn in his shoulder became a fire. Blood poured down his arm from three large gashes. His head swam and he dropped to his knees. The blood had to be staunched. He rooted with his left hand in his sack, and pulled a cloth out with shaking fingers, as pain bloomed through his arm, up his neck and into his head. He groaned through his teeth.

And then a girl knelt in front of him.

She took the cloth and pressed it hard against the gashes.

His vision blurred and he gripped the leaves on the ground, forcing himself to breathe slowly. His sight finally cleared. Large dark glittering eyes gazed at him and golden-red hair in wild tangles framed a small face. Antlers grew from her forehead, branching into three points each.

He pulled in a gasp that had nothing to do with the attack or the pressure on his wound. The roe people were real. As an adult, he'd given no credence to the stories, but here was a girl—a girl with antlers—touching him.

She made a noise like a coo followed by a grunt. Lifting her brows as if she'd asked a question, she stared at him.

"I'm sorry. I can't understand you," he mumbled through the pain.

She shook her antlers, grabbed his hand, and made him hold the cloth in place.

Then she stood and transformed.

Her arms lengthened into front legs, the soft covering that looked like a ragged dress turned into a thick hide, and her bare feet became hooves. It all happened in less than a second and the roe disappeared into the trees.

Stunned, Alek scooted against a trunk and leaned there, panting and holding his arm.

A roe girl. A beauty. A siren of the woods. No wonder there were tales of men wandering into the forest after elusive maidens. Never to return. His arm throbbed. He needed to get up. Needed to get out of here.

He'd made it to his knees when she returned. With one hand, she pushed him back against the tree and moved the cloth out of the way. She smeared something green from her other hand over the gashes. He trembled with the sting of it and the girl cooed again, cocking her antlers to one side.

When she appeared satisfied with her slathering job, she sat in front of him. Her face moved close to his and she breathed deep. Was she smelling him? Her nose bumped his twice and she leaned back, a shy smile tipping up her mouth.

Slowly, he let one finger touch her cheek and then her antler. Her smile got bigger but a cracking sound in the distance made her start. She grabbed him by his good arm and hauled him to his feet with more strength than he expected.

She pulled him along, snorting. Soon they were back where he'd been mapping the route. His string was still tied off. She pointed at it, grunted and growled, and pointed back toward the edge of the forest.

"I know," Alek said. "I shouldn't be here."

She cocked her antlers again. He was starting to find the gesture charming.

"But I'm glad I came into the forest. Even if I did end up with this." He pointed to his arm.

She cooed.

He untied the string and dropped it into his sack. As he fastened it, the roe girl came close to him. She pointed to the edge of the forest once again and touched his injured arm.

Then waved back at the depths of the forest, all the while making her little grunts. She stamped a foot.

"Yeah. I should go." He took her hand. "Thank you for what you did. I'm pretty sure you saved my life."

The roe girl stood on her tiptoes and smelled him again. She rubbed her nose on his cheek and backed up.

Then bolted away.

The last he saw of her was the flash of a white tail.

Alek unrolled the map on the lectern, thankful his arm was finally out of the sling. The leaders of the Carters Guild took their seats, mugs of drink still in hand.

"Well, sir," one bearded old fellow said. "You say you have a report for us, but what's this about you being attacked?"

Alek opened his mouth, but another man piped up. "A treecat? I've never heard tell of anyone surviving a treecat."

"I hadn't either," Alek agreed. "The only reason I survived was because the cat was scared off by another animal."

Murmuring swelled and quieted.

The bearded one said, "Carry on then."

"Before I was attacked, I was able to map out a portion of the route. I used my measurements of that portion to create a conservative estimate for the entire toll road."

He passed the map to the bearded man. "Accounting for the number of trees that would need to be felled, the leveling necessary for carts and wagons, and the large crews that would be required, the project would cost upwards of seven hundred and fifty gold."

Shocked grumbles ran through the men.

"Frankly, sirs," he continued, "even if you could afford to build the road, I imagine you will find it hard to get your carters to use it, much less pay their hard-earned money to do so. I suggest you put it to a vote with your full membership before you proceed."

Outside the public house, Alek sighed with relief as he slipped a coin to the boy he'd hired to eavesdrop on the guild vote. The toll road had been overwhelmingly voted down. The creatures in that corner of the forest could live uninterrupted, at least for now. He'd only been paid a fraction of his fee, which set his credentials back months, if not years. But somehow, the lack of monetary reward didn't bother him as much as it should.

He scratched his shoulder. The scars still itched, but they were healing nicely. The road to his right led out of town, around the forest, skirting its green borders. He paused in the street, staring down the road at the trees. He quickly turned around, back toward his lodgings, one hand resting on his new dagger. He wouldn't be one of the men who was lost to the forest because of a mystery maiden. He was smarter than that.

Again, Alek stood at the edge of the forest, the toes of his boots touching the line between human territory and wild wood. A full beard proved he hadn't shaved in a while and he had complete use of his arm back. His gaze searched, as deep into the trees as the dim light allowed, for any glimpse of antlers or tangled red–gold hair.

No farther, he told himself. This was as far as he would go this time.

Revenge Song

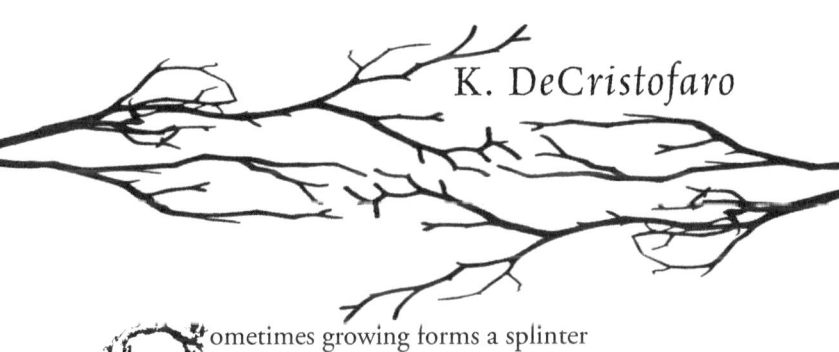

K. DeCristofaro

Sometimes growing forms a splinter
    sometimes learning makes you bleed
    when the ivy has been poisoned
getting sick becomes a need

do you like it
do you cherish
how you're choking on the leaves
of the willow
turned a killer
growing hostile to the breeze

now the roots like strings
are wrapping, snapping
feeble bones with ease
"girl's a psycho"
called me crazy

look how crazy i can be

will the soil
teach you loyalty
once you've been buried deep
cherry stealer
i'm a healer
i'll correct your neck for cheap

do you wish you'd
learned more quickly
do you wish mistakes were free
now you're sinking
and i'm swimming in
these caustic memories

bark is cracking
veins are sapping
you can blame me if you please
but you blew and bent and broke me
what you've sown is what you'll reap

so my love became a splinter
and it's been embedded deep
and the willow that found stillness
will not be the one to weep

Haunted

AudraKate Gonzalez

I wake, drenched in sweat. My head is throbbing, and my body feels even worse. Rolling out of bed, adjusting my eyes to the bright light of the sun, I look back at the empty spot next to me. My wife is already up, which means our daughter probably is as well. That is when the warm scent of stew makes its way to my nose. My stomach grumbles and then I look at my hands, remembering it all. The rust–colored stains that press into my calluses may one day wash away, but the massacre I caused will never be wiped from my mind.

The Night of the Massacre-
The winters in Aregelia are always brutal. The land freezes over and snow drifts down from the mountains, leaving much of our food supply scarce. A few rodents here, a quail every so often, and when you come upon a wolf—that is a real treat. As

a hunter for the King's guard, it is my job to make sure that meat always fills his table, which means his family always comes before mine. No food for the King, no coin for me.

Not that coin does me much good when the markets in the village are low on stock due to trading complications in this weather. The food supply has gotten so bad that the King has even employed the help of a mage. Complete and utter blasphemy to most, but only those in the service of the King know this dark secret and it would be our heads if we ever revealed it. The mage looks into his crystal globes and works his enchantments to locate a food source. When he is given a vision, it is my job to hunt it down and bring it back to the castle.

But I believe his magic to be a ruse because I have come back empty-handed almost every time.

When I last returned to the castle with no meat in my hands, it was me who was blamed. "What kind of a hunter are you that you cannot even locate some measly little quail whose location has been revealed?" I was struck across the face by the mercenary.

"I promise I won't fail again."

"Oh, I know you will not, for the next time you return empty-handed will be the last time you have hands to use."

So, there I was, out in the west woods of Aregelia hunting for the wolf the mage saw in his vision.

"A large wolf you will find, and death will linger close

behind." That was the riddle he had magicked up for me. Whatever it meant, I was not entirely sure. I just knew I needed this wolf more than anything.

The wind blew hard, and I was beginning to lose feeling in my hands, the hands I needed to slay the wolf or forever part with them. The sun was going down and my deadline to find this wolf was at dawn tomorrow. The meat was to be part of a grand feast with other wealthy lords and ladies in the kingdom. I would bring the meat to them, gutted, cleaned, and ready for cooking.

I was losing my temper at the weather conditions around me. The trees were looming above and sticks were hidden under the snow and kept cracking under my feet, ensuring that I would not be able to sneak up on any wolf. If there was even a wolf out there. There was no way for me to find any tracks with all the snow drifting across the paths. The footprints I had just left behind were already covered, as though I had never been there.

I took my hunting knife and started hacking at a large oak tree. It took out my frustration and kept my limbs warm. As I was hacking away, I saw it. Not the wolf, but something. A blur of red streaking through the woods, moving quickly through the trees. My eyes locked on and my body reacted. I went in pursuit. At my age, forty-three winters old, I had to pace my run so I did not burn out early. Pacing myself also helped ensure that my prey would not hear me approaching for the kill.

We kept like this for a while. The red figure moving in front, me following further behind, going deeper and deeper into the woods. Deeper than I had ever traveled. I stopped in my tracks. Another movement caught my eye. Smoke was lifting into the air ahead of me and, through the blizzard of snow and creeping darkness, I saw a cottage coming into view. I had been through these woods many, many times and had never come across this cottage before.

That told me just how deep we had gone. A girl with raven black hair and a cloak crimson in color walked up the stairs and the door opened to her, spilling warm light across the snow.

My biggest regret was that I did not turn around right then. That I did not continue my hunt for the alleged wolf and await my fate at the castle if I never found it. Instead, I followed the young girl into the house.

An old woman stood in a small, drab kitchen. A gasp escaped her when she turned to see me standing in the doorway behind the girl.

"Sorry to intrude. I saw the smoke and was hoping I'd be able to catch a moment's breath in the warmth." I rubbed my hands together, playing the part of a frozen man.

The old woman gestured toward a seat at her table. The girl looked at me warily, but didn't say a word.

"What brings you out to these parts of the wood?"

the woman asked as she scooped a ladle of something warm into a bowl.

"A hunt for the King."

The young girl's eyes widened. "You hunt for the King? What's he like? Have you been inside the castle?" There was awe in her voice.

"Ruby, don't bother the man with your questions. He's on business." The woman placed the bowl of warm liquid in front of me. "You'll have to excuse my granddaughter. She has always fancied the royals."

I nodded. "Unfortunately, I have yet to find what the King is expecting. I was wondering if you folks would be of any assistance. It is important for the King's table to be plentiful." I unsheathed my knife and placed it on the table menacingly. They needed to know that I meant business.

"Sir, I—" The woman blubbered, but I cut her off.

"The King is waiting," I tsked.

Lifting the spoon to my lips, I slurped the liquid loudly as the woman and her granddaughter frantically rushed around to find me morsels to bring to the King. To my disappointment, it wasn't warm broth I sipped, but instead warm water. Slowly, I placed the spoon back into the bowl, realizing that this woman and her granddaughter would have nothing of worth.

When the girl rushed over and handed me what her and her grandmother had—I lost it.

"Sir, this is all we have. It is yours if you wish." She lifted a basket of mold-splotched bread to me. Her gaunt face held back tears I knew she wanted to release. Her grandmother placed an arm around her as she tried to calm her. I wanted to feel sorrow for these two women who welcomed me into their home. Who were kind to me and offered me warmth when I deserved none. But my own fear had arisen as I thought of returning to the castle empty-handed once again. And that was when I picked up my knife and did what I did best. I hunted.

I returned to the castle and was greeted with great applause as I brought back the feast the King so desired. I felt sick to my stomach at the thought, but if I let anyone know what had occurred in those woods, I would be awaiting the gallows in no time. The only one who gave me a cross look at my return was the mage. There was no indication that he knew what had happened, but his shifty glances and low whispers made me nervous. There was no way anyone would ever find out. I scrubbed the cottage clean and buried the bloody clothes in the woods and anything else away from the cottage. I told myself it was just like any other kill, and it wasn't until I tossed that crimson cloak in the makeshift grave that I let any tears spill.

Now here I am, warm at home and I will not be called to the castle again for at least a week. I glance at the stand next to our bed and see the satchel of coins that rest there. More coins than I have received in a while. I wonder how long I can make it last. I do not know if I have the strength to do another hunt again.

"Phillip, breakfast is ready," my wife, Ariel, stands in the doorway. "You look ill. Is everything alright?"

"Fine, my love. Just a bad dream is all."

"Daddy! Daddy! Daddy! Come! You must eat breakfast! I helped Mama make it!" Ella, our daughter, comes bursting into the room with the biggest smile I have ever seen. Despite my mood, I can't help but feel cheered by her innocence. The innocence of a young girl. Innocence that I have taken away from someone else. I blanche. My wife notices.

"Ella, why don't we give your father some time to put himself together." Ariel takes Ella off into the kitchen. I want to follow, but I am going to need a lot more than a few minutes to put myself together.

I can't stomach breakfast. As delicious as it smells, I can't bring myself to swallow stew, so I settle for an apple. I see the disappointment on Ella's face when I say I do not want any stew, and I know I have to make it up to her. So, after breakfast I let her borrow my hunting furs to keep warm, and outside we go. We toss around a few snowballs and make a snowman. When that is all finished, I go chop some firewood and tell Ella she can play in the woods as long as she stays close to where I can see her.

My muscles strain against my clothing as I chop away, making the logs smaller and smaller. Splinters of wood are flying through the air around me. Most of the time I would find the motion of cutting the wood to relax my mind. The sweat that would drip from my brow and soreness that would come later would be a reward. But now, my mind wanders as the motion sends me into a trance. As it sends me back to that cottage. The wood beneath my ax turns to bones. My eyes widen and I try everything I can to stop the ax, but it is too heavy, and its weight is dragging me down. The ax connects. The bone crunches and I can't help but scream. I fall backward onto the ground and a blast of cold air rushes behind me.

I sense someone watching me and I quickly turn around, jumping to my feet. And there she is. The girl with the raven black hair. Her clothing is in tatters. Her pallor matches the snow, like she was robbed of all her blood. I notice stitching across her limbs, and I imagine the Reaper himself putting back together what I had destroyed. She is looking down at her feet, whimpering, and she wipes at her face. My heart feels like it is going to burst, but whether it is from fear or sorrow, I do not know. I reach my hands out to the girl, this phantom, hoping I can help her in death when I did not in life. Before I can touch her, she snaps her head up and gives a wicked, evil smile that steals the breath from my lungs. She lets out a banshee's scream and I'm blown back onto the ground. When I look up, it is like she was never even there.

My eyes are deceiving me. I have not had enough sleep to recover from the evil I had done and my conscience is making me pay for it. As I try to calm my mind, a giggle comes from behind me. A flash of red blurs through the trees. The crimson cloak. I pick up my ax and take off after the spirit. I have guilt in my heart, but I will not let myself be tormented by a ghost. I am racing behind the red cloak, the giggles still sounding in my ears. I reach out and grab the cloak, spinning the girl around to face me. I brandish my ax over my head and notice the terrified eyes that stare back up at me.

"Daddy?" Ella looks at me, tears spilling down her cheeks.

"Where did you find this cloak?" I demand.

"Dadd—"

"Where, Ella?!"

"The girl! The girl gave it to me. She said you would want me to have it!"

My mouth drops open. The ghost had spoken to my daughter. Gooseflesh covers my whole body as I realize what else could have been said to her.

"Did she say anything else to you?!"

"No." And then Ella starts to cry even harder. I rip the

cloak off Ella and throw it out into the woods behind me.

"Phillip! What are you doing?!" Ariel comes storming out of the house at the sound of Ella's outburst. I quickly release Ella. I cannot believe how far I let myself go. How far this spirit pushed me to go. Ella scrambles to her mother and throws her arms around her. Ariel cradles her and looks at me with murderous eyes.

"What were you thinking?" she half screams at me, her voice trying to stay level so as not to frighten Ella any more.

"I—" I can't even mutter a coherent sentence that would explain what I was doing. I cannot let my wife know I am seeing ghosts. Especially not the ghost of a girl I had slain. Ariel does not wait any longer for a response as she pulls Ella along with her into the house and slams the door.

I stay outside for the rest of the day, sitting on the stoop, not being able to bring myself to look at Ariel or Ella. The whole time I sit in the cold, my thoughts race and memories resurface from the night before. I empty whatever contents I may have in my stomach more than once as I picture the blood-soaked cottage and the lifeless eyes staring back at me. I know the girl's spirit is not finished with me. I know I will see her again. With this thought comes the feeling of eyes watching me and it is the only thing that has me dragging myself into the house.

That night, I lay in our bed alone since Ariel decided to

sleep with Ella. Ariel does not wish to speak to me, and Ella is too scared to even look at me. I toss and turn as noises sound throughout the house. A creak there. A scuffle here. I keep my eyes on the doorway waiting for the phantom girl to make an appearance, but hour after hour passes and still nothing. I should just close my eyes and try to find sleep, but every time my eyelids seek rest, I see her grim smile. Rotted teeth peek out from her lips as a slimy black tongue runs across them. My eyes burn as I force them to stay open and I wonder how I am ever going to get through this night. That is when the shadow goes past the doorway and the pitter-patter of feet head toward the kitchen.

I throw off the heavy quilt my wife had made and slowly creep down the hall after the shadow. I stop in the kitchen and scan my surroundings. My eyes try to adjust to the darkness and what little moonlight filters in through the window. I look for any sign of movement. Anything out of place. As I am about to mark everything as normal, I notice the basket sitting in the center of the table. It had not been there before. I step closer to the basket and see the mold-splotched bread. The bread I once turned away is now in a basket on my table, but mold is not the only thing growing on it. Insects of all kinds are crawling all over the bread. Flies swarm out of the basket and hover over the rotting meal. In the center of the basket, between the pieces of bread, is a single finger sticking straight out. The flesh falling off it and onto the bread. My stomach begins to churn, but I have to know if what I am seeing is real.

Leaning over the basket, closer and closer, I reach out to touch it. The bony finger feels rigid and, what skin is left, feels dry and stretched. A gag reaches my throat and I take a step back, but the rest of the hand attached to the rotten finger flies out and grabs my wrist.

I scream and fall backward into the hearth, knocking over a stack of saucers on my way down. The noise must stir Ariel because she is bolting down the hall. She comes in looking around and finally spots me. Unable to move from my terrified position, Ariel places a hand on my arm.

"Are you okay? What happened?" Again, I find myself at a loss for words, so I just point to the table. The table where the basket sits. The table that is now empty. I quickly get up and frantically look around for the evidence that caused my fear, but it is gone. Ariel looks at me with worry in her eyes.

"Let us get you back to bed," she says. But, if sleep was far from me before, it is now permanently out of my reach.

A period of seven nights has passed since the last time I had a full night's sleep. The spirit knows every time I am about to succumb to sleep and she makes sure it never happens. Scratching on the walls, whispering in my ear, and shaking the bed are just a few of the many ways she is slowly driving me mad. The brown scruff on my face has turned into a bush and is becoming grayer by the day.

Food is vile any time I try to eat. It looks and smells delicious, but the moment the spoon reaches my mouth, the food turns sour and is no longer edible. I have lost most of my muscle. My cheeks are sunken, and my eyes are rimmed with dark circles. I look like a crazed man, and Ariel and Ella have become wary of coming near me. They avoid me at all costs, leaving me alone as they go to the market every day and do not return until night is near.

When they left today, I did not bother getting up from the bed to say goodbye to them. The girl has turned me into my own version of the living dead, and I have no desire to do anything. But my wishes to rot away in this bed are crushed when a knock comes at the door. At first I think it must be the spirit again, trying to get another rise out of me, but then I hear a man say, "A message for Sir Phillip Norwell from the Royal Highness, King Jerrick."

I roll my body up from the bed and drag myself to the door.

A royal messenger stands before me dressed in the royal colors of blue and gold, with the King's sigil of a white wolf across his chest. He looks up at me and I can see a startled expression in his eyes at my appearance. He clears his throat.

"The King's mage has had another vision of a wolf in the west woods. The King requests you locate this wolf and bring back the meat to his table in two days' time."

"The west woods?" I nearly groan as the cottage flashes in my mind. "Yes, sir," and with that he turns and leaves.

My stomach sinks as I think about being in the territory where I took the life of the girl and her grandmother. If the girl can haunt me in my own home, I can only imagine how much more she can do to me in those woods. I leave a letter on the table for Ariel and Ella, letting them know where I am going and that I will return within two days, then I set off for the west woods.

The west woods seem a great deal darker to me than they did the last time I was here. The trees loom over me and seem to whisper to each other in the light breeze. Whispers about knowing my sins trickle through their boughs. I know it is my imagination, but I cannot shake the feeling that something sinister is in the works here. I march deeper and deeper into the woods, looking for any signs of a wolf. I feel like my efforts are going to go to waste as I remind myself it is the mage who claims he saw the wolf in a vision. It is hard for me to hunt something that I do not believe exists in the first place, and I remember what happened the last time I became desperate to find something in these woods.

I keep my eyes on the ground as I search for animal tracks. The thick, white snow will make it easier to find something, especially since the weather is mild this evening and the sun is still peeking out in the sky. This is also what makes it easier to spot the droplets of red in the snow. I crouch down and touch the substance. The sticky texture and metallic scent confirm what I already assumed. This is fresh blood. A twig snaps and I freeze, listening to all the sounds around me. A bird somewhere in the distance. A stream to the left of me. A giggle behind me. A *giggle*.

The girl. She looks the same as before, only this time red liquid drips from the crimson cloak wrapped around her. She screams a blood–curdling scream then stops and slowly mouths the word, "Run," and smiles.

It takes me a moment to get my body to listen to me, but when it finally does, I am blindly sprinting through the woods. I can hear footsteps behind me, but I am too afraid to look back.

My chest burns, and my muscles are weak from the lack of sleep and food, but I cannot stop. I will not stop. I do not stop. At least not until I come upon the cottage. I trip over my feet when I first see it, but I remind myself not to get distracted and when I hear the footsteps closer behind me, I take off again.

My arms are pumping. My legs are pushing through the ache. My sides scream at me, but I ignore it all. I am running for what feels like an eternity, but the girl's laughter behind me tells me that I have to keep going. As tiredness begins to set in, I stumble. I land on my hands and knees. I take a few deep breaths to gather some strength and then I feel ready to run again. But, when I go to move, the cottage is in front of me once more.

I move in a different direction and come out on the other side of the cottage. Again and again this happens. No matter where I go, I end up back at the cottage. My eyes water with fury because I have fallen into the girl's trap. She wanted me to come back to the cottage this whole time. Back to the place where I destroyed her life. She stands on the steps of the cottage, and smiles that gruesome smile, then she walks inside the door.

My heart is hammering. I do not know what awaits me on the other side of the door, but I know I have no other choice but to follow after her. I trudge up the stairs, my body shaking at every step. I could say that it is from all the running, but really I know it is from fear. I step inside and the cottage looks like an absolute massacre. It appears exactly the way it did before I scrubbed and scrubbed the floors until my knuckles bled. The turned-over table and chairs, the smashed glass, and the basket with its rotten contents are strewn all over the place. In the center of it all stands the girl with a grim look on her face. A tear rolls down her cheek and I immediately want to repent for everything I did to her. Getting down on my knees, I beg for her forgiveness.

"I'm so sorry. I wish I could take it back. I wish I had just taken whatever punishment from the King. You did not deserve it." Sobs rack my body, and I cannot make my eyes meet her sad stare.

She walks over and brushes a ghostly, cold hand across my cheek, wiping away my tears. I look up at her and she gazes off into the distance. In the smallest whisper, she says, "My, what big teeth you have."

She steps away from me. A look of confusion crosses my face. She is not speaking to me. That gruesome smile appears again, and I feel hot breath on my back. I turn around and there is the wolf in all its glory. Its red eyes gleam at me and saliva drips from its jowls. I am drawn back to the mage's words from before. A large wolf you will find, and death will linger close behind.

Death is not meant for the wolf.

Death is meant for me.

I had caused pain. I had caused suffering. And now it would seem fate is returning the favor unto me. I could try to run from it, but the girl is proof that I will only be tormented for the rest of my days. That no matter how much I try to avoid it, death will always linger near me.

I turn to the girl and bow my head in acceptance. Then I face the snarling wolf and I greet death with open arms. The wolf jumps on me and I let it destroy me. I lie there and let the pain take over. I let the suffering consume me. And when I can hold on no longer, I let the darkness engulf me.

Little Red Monster

Julia Skinner

To those afraid of the history flowing in their veins.

I smell the roses long before the forest comes into view. The sweet, poisonous scent dances across the wind, weaving around me as if it is welcoming me home. As if it is a friend, like it was when I was a little girl.

"Come," it seems to say, "this way! This way!"

But it isn't my friend. And this isn't my home.

Memories of what the roses turned my grandmother into—what it wants me to be—rise in my mind, red and dark.

I will never be your monster.

I want to scream the words. But my voice snags in my throat, choked by the roses' sickly smell. Three years ago, I swore to never return.

But here I am, miles away from any sort of civilization, climbing the last hill that stands between me and the forest my family has watched over for generations.

They're all gone—my family. I am the last.

I finally reach the top of the hill, and my heart stutters in my chest. The forest is so *beautiful*. The pines stand like a wall at the base of the hill. A cacophony of perfumed mysteries twine around their boughs.

Home.

Home.

Home.

The word thuds in my mind, matching the pace of my heartbeat. I can almost feel the wind on my face as a younger me races through those shadows. I can almost hear the cracking of branches beneath my bare feet. Feel the scent of roses wrap around me like velvet arms. Tears blur my vision.

But quickly, images of bloodied fangs replace those few happy memories.

I dig my too-sharp nails into the palms of my hands. *This is. . . this is not home.* This is the place I hate. This is the place of thorns and nightmares and monsters.

I'm not here because I miss it.

I'm not here because everytime I smell the scent of flowers, I can feel the forest calling me.

I am not here because of the beast imprisoned inside of me.

I am here to save the only father figure I've ever had. The only person who has ever cared about me.

That's it.

Sucking in a deep breath, I start down the hill.

I deserve this, I told myself furiously. Cold seeped through the cloak, melting into my skin. This way, I can't hurt anyone.

Heavy footsteps halted at the mouth of the alley. I peeked over the brim of my torn cloak. A hulking man filled the entrance. Dark sideburns with a mix of white lined the sides of his cheeks. He balanced an axe against his shoulder.

I dropped the edges of my cloak, and curled my hands into fists, nails piercing my palms.

"This isn't a place for a kid," he rumbled. He had the kind of voice a boulder would have, if a boulder could speak. "Where's your family, girlie?"

"Don't have one." Annoyance prickled the back of my neck. If I was in my true form, he would already be dead. "Go away."

He chuckled. "How about I help you find somewhere better to stay?"

"No."

"Why not?"

"I'm a monster. You don't want to mess with a monster."

Unexpectedly, the man tipped his head back and released a booming laugh. I jumped, then scowled, chapped lips curling around my fine-tipped teeth. He thought I was too young, too small to be dangerous. Bitterness clawed my throat.

"Well, Little Monster, it's a pleasure to meet you. My name's Paul."

He waited for a response. When I didn't give one, he left without another word.

And that's that, *I thought.*

But the next day he returned with food.

Food—*as if he was attempting to pacify a feral animal. Maybe he was. Driven by the sharp ache in my gut, I accepted it. As I ate, he talked about the techniques of woodcarving.*

I listened, but I didn't let him know it.

Weeks passed like that. Me eating. Him talking. Sometimes he would get a few words from me. Sometimes not.

But one day, he sat down and said, "I could give you a job. You could be my apprentice, if you wanted."

I stared at him, astonished. No one had ever wanted me for anything. Not even my grandmother. Slowly, though, I shook my head.

"Why not?" he asked.

"I'm a monster."

I might hurt you one day.

"Would you like to know a secret?" He glanced down at the axe he always carried, then back at me. "A monster is only a monster if they choose to be. Do you want to be a monster?"

I didn't answer. Couldn't. My throat was too tight. My grandmother's voice too loud and scathing and accusing in my memories. For as long as I could remember, she had told me who I was, what I was.

A monster.

A monster.

A monster.

Born to kill.

Born to hurt.

I squeezed my eyes closed. "You don't know that," I whispered.

"I do."

"How?"

"Because I wasn't always a woodcarver."

I looked at him, at the lines of his suntanned face, the faded scar peeking from just beneath his left sideburn. And I saw something I had been missing, hidden behind the twinkle in his dark eyes.

A monster.

Different from mine, but a monster all the same.

"You—" but I didn't finish. The word stayed hanging in the air between us, a question and an accusation.

A shadow fell over his face. "Aye." He paused, then sighed. "When I was younger, I was part of a . . . group. We did a lotta bad things. People got hurt."

"So, you were a bandit?" I said.

He cleared his throat. "Uh, yeah. But I'm not that man anymore."

"What changed?"

"Well, I realized I wanted something better. So I ran away from that life. In a way, I'm still running. One day, my sins will probably catch up. You don't just walk away from men like the ones I lived with. But I'm finally happy, y'know?"

My throat tightened, but this time it wasn't from fear, it was hope.

"Anyway," he grunted, "I figured we monsters should stick together."

For the first time in a long time, I smiled.

I stop at the edge of the forest. Here is the border between light and darkness. Freedom and chains. A soft wind blows through the trees, brushing my ragged, tangled hair with the forest's telltale floral scent. No one would know by looking at it from the outside that there is a garden of bright red flowers at the center.

No one knows that that garden—the roses—binds my family here. A curse that turns us into monsters, one by one.

Paul had been right. His sins did finally catch up, and they want his head for betraying them. He thinks. . . he thinks the protector of this place will stop the bandits, that it will save him. He doesn't know that there is no monster to devour his foes. Not anymore. Not since my grandmother died, and I ran away.

Tears burn in my eyes.

I was too afraid to admit it. To tell him.

My body starts to shake as I stare at the edge of the woods, imagining myself stepping over it. If I don't go in, the bandits will find Paul, and they will kill him.

But if I do, I will become everything I vowed I'd never be.

I tipped my head back, and closed my eyes. And there's my grandmother, lurking in the shadows of my mind. Grey hair wisps around her shriveled frame. A jagged scar leers across her right eye. Familiar panic flares through my body as images of flashing fangs and crimson cloaks jolt through my mind. But I don't run, like I did all those years ago.

The memory of my grandmother tilts her head, and smiles. Just as she did the very afternoon she died. It isn't a nice smile, like Paul's. It is sharp and sly, like the shifting shadows that live beneath the pines.

"You know who you are," she told me that day, voice guttural like the snarl of a rabid dog. *"Genie Woff, Cursed monster of this forest. That's all you've ever been. All you will ever be."*

The rancid fear in my gut rises in my throat. I barely swallow it back down.

"A monster is only a monster if they choose to be," Paul's voice fills my mind. My heart thuds, thuds, thuds. *"Do you want to be a monster?"*

I open my eyes, and face the forest that has haunted my nightmares for years. I inhale the sharp scent of roses.

"No," I say loudly. Boldly. Just like Paul always spoke.

I *never* wanted to be a monster.

That's why I ran away.

But maybe that's why I'm back, too. Because only a monster would leave Paul alone to die.

A faint wind brushes past me, bringing with it a different scent. A rotten trace of dirty clothes and sharpened steel.

Bandits.

Something feral squeezes in my chest. A fury that snarls inside of me, nearly uncontrollable. The smell reminds me of the alley I lived in before Paul found me. I bare my teeth.

They're going to kill him, just like Grandmother would have.

I lift my chin. "I don't have to be a monster," I snarl. In my mind, I am saying it to my grandmother. "I can protect. I can choose!"

Just like Paul.

I step forward, across the border. As I do, fear I have carried for so long lifts from my shoulders. The scent of red roses swarms me joyously, thickening until I can almost see it tinting the air crimson. I let it in, let it wrap velvet arms around me. In a few heartbeats, it transforms me into the curse, shifting my body into the form of a giant wolf with red fur and sharp fangs.

The terror of the forest.

And it feels *right*.

Muscles bulging, I pad forward. At the forest's center,

below the canopy of pine limbs, the roses twine together, vining across the ground and up the gnarled trunks. Scarlet petals are scattered on the dark earth, like drops of blood.

Past their sweet smell, the stark, bitter scent of the bandits surrounding their victim stings my nostrils. But they won't touch him.

Not in my woods.

Forest Gods

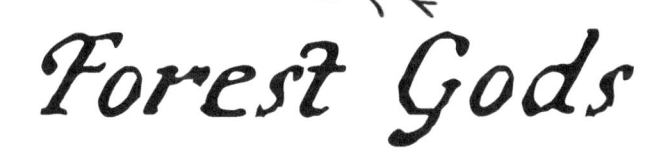

Nathaniel Luscombe

The smell of decay
lingers thick,
polluted air
not renewed
by waking day.
A black forest,
fungi spreads,
fingers of death
buried in soil
rotten and torn.
It has seen me.
It has heard my
heavy breathing,
has smelled my
fear-wetted skin.
It is standing,

antlers scraping
high branches.
The forest gods
have come for me.
Pray they will
let me live.

The Breathing Woods

Xanna Renae

Sophy refused to discover if what she stepped over was a finger or a tree root. Half a mile into the Breathing Woods meant there was no possible way for the ordinary person to know the difference. But this land moved with so much of her own magic that she couldn't mistake one for the other. She did her best to avoid looking now.

More than enough corpses littered the woodland through the years for Sophy to realize that though the woods kept them living, they did not keep them whole. They lay there, the bodies. All without the signs, or smell, of death. But that did not leave them unchanged.

Nature sought to reclaim these lives. But it was not allowed to here. So, nature took what it could.

Only three bodies remained pristine and they were deep in the heart. And she aimed to change that.

Something moaned off in the distance. Stones sank in her

stomach, pulling the organ into the rest of her bowels. Her legs froze where she stood, rooting her feet into the rustling leaves that scampered about the forest floor. She knew what the sounds meant. A new arrival. Whoever those cries belonged to had not lingered long enough for her butchered healing spells to numb their pain.

She turned toward the direction of the cry. Then slowly extended the iron lantern she carried outward, she waited. The cry sounded again. Mortal and full. There was still time for them. She wanted to save them. Once they were calmed and soothed they would become—*no*. She refused to give heed to the rest of that thought. Couldn't allow herself to play the hero again. Nothing good came from it. Muscles in her free hand contorted until it became a fist. Fingernails dug into her palm, threatening to draw blood. There was no right granted to her for dragging people from where they rested to outside the treeline so they could die. She had no say in the matter. Yet.

Pushing off to walk again was a difficult decision. But it was for the best.

Eventually, the cries faded.

A cold wind pushed her back toward where she came. It cut through her clothes and whipped her hair. It smelled of clove and rot. Magic was displeased with her machinations. It favored the will of the master which had stayed. The thought stung.

On she went.

Phantom aches pulsated in the heels of her feet. Wandering around this long demanded a toll be collected. The surrounding magic assuaged most all sensations. It was so annoying. Her destination was hiding from her. . . again. The grove shifted and slithered about. Presumably designed to wear her out by the time she arrived at its heart. Weaken her spirit and mind so she would leave faster than she came.

Sophy hated that she was treated as an unwelcome guest. Did her own will not also flow in the sap of these trees, hold fast to the roots of flowers, and keep death at bay beneath the canopy of brown leaves? She kept the woods alive as much as he, yet they despised her.

Could it sense that she wanted to lift such 'blessings' out of the dirt and soil? Purge the rivers of bark and bone of magic. Splice the rotted arteries. Set nature back to order.

It was unfair. This was for the best. It was *right*.

The world spun. Something caught her ankle, cracking the joint and stealing her shoe as her body lurched forward. Sophy dropped the lantern to catch herself on the ground with her forearms. Her leg landed in a twisted heap against a rather peculiar tree root. Metal stabbed her thigh. The lantern remained lit, though the oil-fed flame staggered.

"Gah, such a warm welcome." She spoke through a tightened throat. Maneuvering onto her side did not prove difficult. Thankfully the pain only lasted a brief moment before it was swallowed by the forest. She hiked her skirt up until her undergarments were barely covered. The knife strapped to her thigh had come loose. In doing so, the blade's edge grazed her skin.

No blood welled from the wound. Simply a scratch. She slipped her shoe back on, then pushed her weapon back down into the sheath and refastened the metal clasp. It was an unfortunate addition required to travel today. But words had proven vain.

A patch of moss curled around her foot. Slowly the tendrils consumed her appendage then released her and settled as a small puddle beside her lanturn. Sophy crawled on her hands and knees to investigate the green bit of life. It was more vibrant than anything else she had seen in this area. It bathed in the yellow light that was cast across the ground, which did not spread far from the glass windows before being swallowed by shadows.

She reached a curious finger out toward it. The moss twisted in on itself when touched. Green wisps evaded being known—but they were so soft. She couldn't resist trailing her fingers through the patch as if it were a cat. It sprang back to fullness immediately after she drew her hand away. The fragrant scent of bright and living earth covered her senses.

"Funny little thing, you are." An equally soft laugh escaped her. "Can you lead me to your master?"

The moss did not move away. Simply circled around her feet.

"Can you lead me to your other master? Please. To him." She traced her finger down the path of packed dirt away from herself. The moss followed slowly before extending beyond her reach—crawling along the ground. A lingering piece of kind, living magic. How long had it wandered alone? Hopefully looking for some way to be useful. Perhaps it recognized the remains of her in itself?

The little moss guide refused to be rushed. No matter how quickly she walked, it kept to a constant crawl. Sophy would have to follow whatever pace the creeping fibers set for her. After all, it was doing her a favor. Trailing to the heart of the woods as a vein would.

Memories came crashing back. She knew the path she took all too well now. It was the very one taken the first time they came here. The light metallic scrape of armor and clanking potion bottles rushed into her mind. The weight of her old healer's pack settled onto her shoulders. She had not used its leather body in years. The worn straps used to be a comfort. A reminder that she could try and save that which was almost lost.

She had thought that when walking this path. Trailing to a tyrant's end, just as she did now.

No. She shook her head. Not a tyrant.

Petrichor permeated through a fog which lilted between

the tree trunks and over open graves. They were motionless, the bodies. Sophy was surprised to see some had actually lowered into the earth here. Most people who dragged their soon-to-be-departed loved ones simply left them somewhere near a worn path close to the treeline. She would come across them propped up nicely against a tree or lying still in a glade. Easy spots to find once their relatives returned to speak of medicines and cures.

Until they stopped coming and left their living-dead to rot.

Bodies weren't a problem. They were resigned to live out their death in the same spot. Slowly morphing into something the woods designed. Some of them became features of the wood itself. Saplings, broken branches, a small pond or creek.

After the battle the forest witnessed, wherein her mismatched adventuring party slayed the tyrannical plague of monsters, the healing magic poured out and refused to let anything die. That lent the thick canopy space its name: The Breathing Woods. Everything that should be dead yet breathed. Time-blessed parents with silvered hair, suckling little ones too young to learn of their fate. They all resided here. Never taking breath themselves. Stuck.

Sophy ducked under a low, fallen maple branch. The bark was lined with little mushrooms and curling flowers. The snapped end of the limb bled water and sap down the length of the tree. Golden and beautiful. A box owl called somewhere off in the deep.

There were no reminders here. A few moments of stillness cleared the fear that clung to her lungs and sternum.

A spared look upward gave her no view of the stars. The thick clouds blanketing the sky would not give the blessing of direction. Only bits of cutting moonlight illuminated her path alongside her lanturn. Only adding to the unsettling nature of the place. That wasn't enough to turn her back. She needed to be here. A visit was long overdue. One could only run so far from the other half of their heart.

The moss stretched itself thin. Soon, it stopped altogether.

"Thank you for guiding me." Sophy knelt down, mindful not to crush the moss with her skirt-covered knees, and placed a light kiss at the end of the trail. "You can return to your lovely little spot now."

The moss pulsed, then recoiled.

And then she was alone again. All alone. And she knew where she was.

The land was mostly barren here for a short mile or so. Husks littered the ground. She didn't want to imagine what they looked like when life flowed through them. It was almost impossible to distinguish between what was natural here—trees and bushes—and what was flesh and bone. Each crunch under her feet pushed bile up into her mouth. She swallowed it back down.

"Breathe, Sophy. Breathe. You're all right." Her jaw trembled as she muttered the words over and over again.

It only took a few minutes to steady herself mentally. Physically, she was fine. It was disconcerting not to feel the fatigue of walking as long as she had. To not truly feel her lungs expand with air or the solid pounding of a heart beneath her breast. This was the realm of the Changed. It's where the transformed dwelled.

She counted backward from thirty as she entered the barren stretch. Each step she took, numbered. Lefts were odd, rights were even.

Trees stood charred and leafless. Bushes and grass grew brown and black. As far as Sophy knew, no animals lived here. The path before her was one created ages ago. Worn down and neat despite the wildness the rest of the wood held.

She kept her eyes trained forward and slightly down.

Five. Four. Three. Two. One.

Living trees surrounded her once again.

Her shoulders relaxed backward.

A body dropped in front of her. A scream welled up in her throat. Sophy had to bite her lips to keep herself from screeching. Its face inches away from her own as it hung down from a tree. Most of their features were gone—as if someone took a painter's brush coated in oil and tried to smear away any definition. No place for eyes or nose, though the recesses remained.

Its jaw cracked and popped open. Sophy did her best not to vomit or reach for the knife strapped to her leg. The flesh around what had to be the thing's mouth began to thin, stretching so only a thin layer of fascia outlined what would have been a wide smile. It grew until the vaguest idea of a void made an attempt at sound.

"Hello," Sophy spoke. "I am here to see the master."

It continued to smile and sway in front of her on a nonexistent breeze. Just a happy child of the woods. Happy for a guest, happy for a light. Happy to think for a moment it was saved. Sophy took in the details she could as she waited. It was draped in rags. Old and tattered and worn and falling apart. They hardly covered the creature's body, which bore no indication of sex. Being this far into the forest, and this filled with magic, it may have been one of the first persons brought here after the battle that had laid siege.

That's right. Person, not creature. Though, was it correct to call such a twisted thing a person? Had it retained all its memories while bounding through the trees, becoming something so... She swallowed. Person. Creature. *Thing*. What was it? Could it really think? Was thinking what made up a person?

Sophy wouldn't brush past them, no. Disrespect could only end in disaster. She would have to wait for it to realize she couldn't save them.

And eventually it did.

The swaying was the first to stop, the fingers spread wide and waggling now curled into small fists. Soon after the creature's jaw crunched shut.

It curled back into the trees, shaking a few leaves as it went.

Sophy hated being a disappointment.

Her fingernails scraped on the iron handle of her light. The sound produced was vomit inducing. Sophy's body squeezed in on itself, as if trying to dispel the sound and disappointment from her very soul. If only such a thing were possible. But oh how she tried to free them. To snip the veins tethering these beings to life. Unable to pull the trapped souls out of the wood's shelter to allow them to pass on, all Sophy could do was regret and walk forward.

Something hit her from behind. Her knees folded under her contorting body and Sophy landed on the ground in a heap. The gnarled bits of trees hadn't scraped her arms or legs. She groaned and pushed herself back up, breaking into a half sprint as she evaded whatever struck her. She wanted to cut through the rest of the muscle that surrounded the heart. To be rid of the fears that lingered and draped through the trees.

She blindly charged forward, her lantern extended straight outward. She stumbled occasionally but somehow remained upright. No longer stopping to examine the suffering world around her. There was enough torture. It was time to start avoiding the need to look at all that was ensnared.

A burst of green filled her vision. The air glowed with golden strands of light woven through thick canopies of olive leaves. Sophy froze, not yet stepping through the thickets and tall grass. The sky above was clear, allowing the moon to bathe the area. Leaves rustled softly as a breeze danced with them. The soft buzz of little bugs came next.

It was time to face them all.

"*Sophy*, you return to us once more. See her approach? Truly our healer. Meek and out of breath. I heard her racing through the trees. Felt her feet strike earth." A deep voice called from the other side of the glade. There he sat with the others in a bed of flowers. His arms moved about, but he did not turn to greet her, nor did he stop his puppeteering. "Have you discovered something new from out there in the world you spend so much time in? Anything for us to try?"

Sophy set her lantern by the entrance to the glade, making certain it wouldn't tip and spill a blaze upon the flora and fauna.

"Arden," Sophy murmured as she approached. "You know well I have stopped looking. There is nothing to find." Tall grass speckled with red brushed against her legs and skirt. She paused a few paces away from him, taking in the only being that was allowed to change here.

Arden's hair had grown longer. The chestnut color ran down his spine and pooled around his hips.

"Only addressing me? That is right. You have given up on them." He faced her, a tight grin stretching his mouth. Darkness bled down his cheeks from his eyes. Cracks lined his bloodied lips. He had lost some luster in his sharp face. Her stomach warmed and twisted. It would return soon enough.

Sophy closed the gap between them. Slowly walking over fallen blades and snapped arrows.

"It is cruel how you remind me of times passing." His head lulled to the side, an arm reached backward in the grass to hold his relaxed posture upright. Amber eyes pierced her soul. "But crueler yet would I be to relinquish my hold." He returned his gaze to the other three members of their party.

Young fighters lay in a bloodied heap amid brilliant poppies and hellebore, their heads close to each other as the rest of their body stretched outward in cardinal directions. Arden's seated form made up the final point. This was the group before they sought out a healer. Four unlikely friends banded together with the common goal of saving the continent from a growing evil. Four amazing fighters. And though Arden's speciality with blood magic allowed him access to all forms of spellwork, his healing skills were quite lacking.

That's when she came along. She healed him and the others after a particularly nasty fight on her city's outskirts. She'd muttered her healing spells and blushed while she bandaged his naked chest. He'd blushed as he questioned her about her magic skills. Stammered as he asked about her life. Smiled when he asked her to travel with them as their official mage and healer.

"Not even going to look at them, are we?" His voice took on a demeaning tone.

Sophy clamped her lips between her teeth and turned her head.

The girl's ginger hair was clumped up with stems and leaves. Behind her lids Sophy knew there would be a brilliant set of honey eyes. Bright with determination.

Dull with death.

Beside the ginger woman were two men, identical in face. The plated armor affixed to their frames still shone just as bright as it had at the start of their battle ages ago, though it was peppered with bits of blood and dirt. Their boots were soaked red.

All three of their heads were surrounded with crowns of flowers, some crudely woven while others showed a glint of forming talent. Arden was slowly getting better at the craft she taught him.

"I suppose you're going to ask me to leave." Arden's voice scraped low. "You always open with that." His hands began weaving a new crown. Little yellow and red poppies rapidly sprouted from the ground when plucked. Ever replacing what was lost, keeping things as still as possible.

"You seem to forget the years I spent searching and aiding you without question. We do still share a common goal, Arden. We want peace for them." Sophy nodded at and looked upon her fallen friends' forms. "For the last several centuries you've said you would never leave them. To never let them pass as nature wishes. Answer and goal unchanged." A soft breeze swept through the glade as it always did at this point in the conversation.

"I won't." His voice cracked. Deep lines formed on his face, expression growing tense. "I will not allow dirt and roots to claim what should have lived on in my stead." His lips curled, baring his sharp teeth. A touch of black bled into the amber of his eyes.

Good. She preferred him angry for their meetings. It was easier to manage him in this way.

"Then today. . . I will not ask it of you. I will not labor on about the bodies which litter the ground. Nor the changes in the world outside the woodland edge that I wish you would enjoy alongside me." Her voice cracked as she finished. The nerves in her hand twisted toward the blade on her leg. There was still time. Perhaps he would hear her this time.

"And yet, in claiming not to do so, you do." He turned his gaze downward, face unreadable. Hands stilled. He carefully settled the poppy crown in between all three of her old fighting companions. "Can we finish this quickly, please? My friends don't need to hear you speak of their demise." He stood and roughly pushed past Sophy as he stalked to the opposite end of the clearing.

Counting back from thirty calmed her enough to follow.

"They are still my friends as well, Arden. But. . . I cannot help but feel that you've forgotten our bond."

"Our bond is *nothing* when compared to what we should have with them. You return for a purpose. Only ever stating our 'bound duty.' How could I forget when you always remind me that you're still here and they are not. Never able to enjoy what has grown between us? Sophy, they should be able to rejoice in our union. It was only founded to save them." Sourness stabbed with each of his words. The hits landed. She gripped the front of her skirt.

It was true.

What was there to enjoy? Her life was braided with his own, yet it did not create bubbles of pleasure and joy as it ought. All it made her was a shackle around his ankle. A bond such as theirs could only be formed with tied emotions. In all her research, nothing ever specified what emotions were needed. Sophy followed slowly behind him until her shoes brushed up against bloodied dirt.

Arden glared back at her, arms crossed over his middle. The fingers on his right hand began to tap.

She fumbled with the buttons closing the top of her high-neck blouse.

"How unfair is it that mine own enchantments refuse to sustain me as it does them and you." His sentiments always grew poisonous in this spot while their feet sunk into the ground soaked in his own blood. It was far from the sorrowful cries he made as he bled his own magic into the forest floor. The anguish as he slit his arms and begged his spells to keep Hazel and Roth and Jack breathing at the expense of his own life. To save the party he so desperately loved from rotting away.

Except his own offering wasn't enough. He needed to pour out more and more. And so Sophy offered up her own. She recited the same healing spell Arden had as he bit into her shoulder, quickly spilling her blood.

Nature listened to their cries then. Granting Arden's wish in the twisted fashion it willed.

The roots soaked in his blood and took his life, as much as he was able to give, and it kept them all alive. It froze the forest from that moment onward.

She finally unfastened the button at the middle of her sternum. The shirt billowed open slightly, from just under her chin down to her heart. Arden pinched the fabric at her neck and pulled it over her shoulder, revealing half of her entirely.

She pushed her hand against him as he stepped even closer. "I have yet to give up on them. As I said, Arden, I still wish for their peace. Why must they remain? Lingering in such a state. Their souls need to pass forward. Who knows what they experience as they lay in your bed of flowers." She bit her lip, almost drawing blood herself as she found the courage to speak again. Changing his mind was impossible. Why was it so impossible? Why were her words never enough? "While they lay there, peaceful and calm, what agony takes place in their trapped spirits? I see it in the people here. How they all rot until the woods claim them and form them into unspeakable monsters begging to be freed. How they beg me, Arden."

"I do not care for the rest of the beings that wind up here. Ergo, they become what they are. They," he pointed behind her with sharp articulation, "do not suffer. I will not allow it. So it cannot be."

"How do you know that's true?" Her glare did nothing to move Arden.

He simply stared at her with disapproval and disdain. It was clearly written in the scrunch of his nose, the curl of his lips, and the glare forged in his own eyes. "How could you give up on them? Our magic combined did this. Think of what more it could do if you had not stopped trying, Sophy!" Grave was his voice, cutting low into the soil to set such fear into her.

She responded as softly as she could, hoping to appeal to his wanted sense of humanity. "What life would they return to, Arden? Tell me. What life could we provide for them now?"

Long fingers knotted into the hair at the back of her scalp, his nails scraping against skin as his grip forced her head backward. Her gasp caught in her throat. All she could see was stars.

"I grow tired of your speaking, Sophy. This conversation is finished." His other slender arm snaked around her middle, holding her upright as his teeth ripped into her.

Time did not pass as he drank. His magical aura spun in the air surrounding them, quickly replenishing her marrow for him to consume. Dizziness would not come. Fatigue would not come. Peace would not come. She could stand here an eternity and still he would drink. Yet still she would give. Her heart sang as he consumed her.

She couldn't get lost in the euphoria.

One of his fingers traced a light circle against her spine. She doubted that Arden realized he was doing it. It signaled his mind slowly relaxing, his gathering strength.

"You have to let go at some point," Sophy murmured. "I grow tired of this forceful taking of yours."

He muttered something incomprehensible. The movement allowed blood to pour from his mouth and stain her breast. But they'd had the conversation enough times for her to have memorized the script. Which meant it was time to try something new.

Sophy went limp as a rag doll. Arden's arms tightened around her middle, his body lurching forward as her weight dragged them down. His maw held fast to her neck. A warning growl slipped past. He did not have patience with her.

She snaked a hand under her skirt and up her leg until she met leather. As quickly as she pulled the knife from its holder she shoved it between Arden's ribs and ripped it out through his side. An arc of blood sprayed the flowers surrounding them.

He unclamped his jaw and stumbled backward, hands now clutching his weeping side. Blood poured out of his mouth. "What do you hope to gain with such a betrayal? To annoy me?" He spat at her. Amber eyes flashed black in the moonlight. "You know wounds like this cannot kill me. It doesn't even hurt. Do you only seek to anger me? Because trust me, I am beyond angry."

Her chest heaved, blood pouring down her neck. "You're half fed, Arden." She raised the blood soaked tip at him. "Running on instinct at this point. If you want to have your fill, you'll have to catch me."

His thin brows knit together. "What are you saying?" The muscles in his face twitched, and the whites of his eyes clouded black.

He would frenzy if she failed.

Sophy threw the blade. It landed with a wet thunk in the center of his stomach. With wide eyes Arden gripped the hilt and pulled it free. He sputtered something. An unsteady stagger set in his step. She watched him intently as his jaw quivered. The wound began to close. Slowly. He'd fed just enough.

Perfect.

Sophy turned and darted out of the glade. The thickets encasing the area attempted in vain to hold her. As much as Arden's will controlled them, it wouldn't allow harm to come upon her, and thus released her. The bite on her shoulder continued pouring blood as she hiked up the skirt of her dress and crawled over a fallen trunk. Its half-rotted trunk groaned underneath her weight.

Trees and plants rustled behind her. She looked back. Arden's frame sluggishly followed, his body no longer used to the level of activity. That would change as soon as he began absorbing what he'd consumed. How quickly her blood revitalized him was astonishing.

Branches scraped along her flesh. Shapeless things moaned as she sprinted past them. Around the bend of trees. Over the gnarled bushes.

"Sophy!" Arden's voice grew in strength and desperation. "*Sophy!*" Anger. Same as the day she first walked away without the intention to return.

Decades went by as she roamed the world which lay outside the trees. All spent waiting for the magics to develop a spell or potion or medicine that would revive and save their fallen friends.

Only one of them could leave the woods at a time to keep the healing intact. Sophy, being the scholar she was, was the logical choice to go off in search. So she wandered and wandered until the pull of the bond in her heart led her back to Arden so he could feed. The man whose life was intertwined with her own for eternity onward. She would relay unto what she had learned. He would drink while she spoke, his fingers rubbing circles against her hips. Then, they would try every idea brought. But nothing worked.

Nothing ever worked.

Slowly, Arden's greetings lost their warmth. He withdrew faster from their embraces.

Slowly Sophy found it easier to leave him than to return to them, until today. Today she entered with the determination to bring life back to her other half. To return him to herself whole and unbroken. To lay their comrades to rest.

The rustling behind her grew in intensity. Clearly Arden now had the strength to better navigate and close the gap that grew between them. If only emotionally as well as physically.

She pumped her legs faster, ignoring the darkness that swallowed the edges of her vision. Death could not come for them here. Nor could they die anywhere beyond the forest's reach. They were two souls tied in blood who were unable to be broken in such a manner as bleeding.

A pulse tremored the ground. Her mouth ran dry. She pushed her legs harder. Harder. If she could pull him out of the forest alongside herself, the magic would snap. They'd be free—together.

Light filtered through the leaves above her. The trees thinned in front of her. The ground hard beneath her. Rocks and roots tore at her back as her frame slid against the ground. The weight of Arden's body pinning her down.

"Enough." He hissed before tearing into her again. Waves of pain coursed down her spine. How? How was he hurting her? Nothing he had ever done had brought her physical pain—

He had never tried harming her, though. Had never raised a hand or any of the weapons at his disposal. Did he feel the knife as she stabbed him? Guilt swam in her gut. She didn't want to bring him pain—not truly.

She scratched at his back and head. Grabbed fistfulls of hair and pulled until his neck arched backward. "Stop fighting me, Sophy. You cannot win. I will not leave without them." He glared down at her, blood spilling from his mouth and drenching her exposed middle.

"You are so willing to forget the living for the dead. It is as if you wish I were the only one gone so that you could roam the world freely with them. Forgetting our bond. Everything we ever dreamed to build has been shattered by time."

Her body erupted with fire. The hilt of her knife stuck out from under her ribs. She coughed, blood escaping her own mouth, coating her tongue in copper. She could feel it. Feel the metal pierce her body. Feel muscle separate from bone. The pressure from the bleeding wounds was agonizing. He ripped the blade from her stomach and slammed it into her thigh, into her shoulder, into her chest, her arms, legs, over and over and over and *over and over and over.*

A scream finally burst from her, accompanied by a spray of blood across his face.

Arden slowly slipped the knife into her stomach one last time. "What?" His voice was cotton fuzz. "You screamed, you, you. . . felt that? Did you feel that—you're hurt? I hurt you." The black frenzy in his irises dissipated. The color was replaced by a reddening, indicative of tears yet to form.

Her pain faded into a buzzing noise. Nothing made sense. Arden gently plucked her from the ground and carried her back to the glade. They passed the Changed without a moment to spare. She thought she saw misery mirrored in their eyes. Saw them recognize how their master would do nothing for them.

Slowly, the world returned. Arden hovered above her. His gaze downcast, lower lip worried by his tongue. He spared a sideways glance at her. She could feel herself bleeding still. The torn muscles of her body twitched every so often. Arden's hands cradled her face, thumbs brushing her cheeks.

He lowered her down into a clean patch of grass in their glade. Away from the blood soaked ground of their arguments, away from the figures of their friends, away from the piles of dust that were once the monsters they sought to destroy.

He threw the knife somewhere deep into the bushes. The only signs of his having been stabbed were a few red lines on his middle. She tilted her head down and screamed. Arden's hand quickly covered her mouth as she saw the gaping wounds. Her skin was marred beyond recognition. Bones stuck out at odd angles, flaps of muscle and flesh twisted up in the folds of her shirt and skirt. Her legs were slick with blood, dirt, and grass.

"Shh, shh, I'm sorry, I'm so *sorry*!" He pressed his hand harder on her open mouth. The force behind it cracked her jaw. "I can heal you." He kept a fist tight against her lips as he cradled her body to his lowered head. He licked at all of her wounds while whispering spells against her skin. Her marred flesh knit itself together with each lap of his tongue. By the time he reached her legs there was no will in her left to scream or cry. Her body couldn't even shake from the shock of it all.

As gently as he healed and held her, he drank. Ever taking.

She was right back in the glade. Trapped under him. It used to feel so safe, being held by his arms. Her memories of their happier times were hazy.

Sophy would lift a hand and play with the strands of hair on the back of his head. Twisting them around her fingers. He'd smile against her neck, maybe chuckle.

All she wanted was to press her nose into his hair and smell the florals that lingered from the ages he's sat amongst them. To ask him the thoughts he's had sitting between the stems and petals. She wanted a moment of his time again, and for that moment to stretch into moments.

She couldn't move her arms. Sensation still registered in her mind, the pressure of Arden's body and grip, the itchy blades of grass, sharp rocks.

Sophy tried moving any part of her, anything. Toes, fingers, a leg. She couldn't even engage the muscles in her stomach.

"Ar-den," she gasped.

He refused to answer her.

"Ar-"

His hand pressed against her mouth, his fingers practically pinching her vocal cords shut.

Something yellow towered over her left eye. A poppy. Little poppies crawled up her sides, tickling her bruising sides. Stocks of hellebore wove around her thighs and wrists.

She was pinned.

Arden withdrew once he obtained enough life to keep his magic flowing. As he wiped his mouth with the back of his hand, his lips were no longer cracked. The dark circles around his eyes lessened in their intensity. Now he looked down at her, sated, full, and tired. "Sophy, I just… just need more time."

And then came the tears. They streamed down his face, tinged pink from all the blood. They stained his skin and clothes as they fell. Quickly they turned into violent sobs. His fists beating the ground beside her body while he screamed. Blood and spit spattered onto her face and chest.

"Why won't you help me? Why do you always leave—you leave and, and you don't come back for so long!" The force of his voice flattened the grass surrounding them.

Her heart pounded against her ribs, threatening to break bone to escape.

Her mutterings were drowned out by his cries. She didn't even know what she would try and say to him.

Arden buried his head on her chest as he continued to sob. Sharp fingers curled into the bones of her shoulders.

The moon stood watch above them. A wide eye capturing every detail. It remained there, motionless.

Her jaw quivered. Spit pooled in the back of her throat. Her lungs attempted to cough, to dispel the fluid. She couldn't move. While she didn't need to breathe, the sensation consumed her. It built until it touched the back of her teeth. Burned into her nasal passage. No. She couldn't even make a sound like this. Gagged silent by her own spit.

Tears streamed down her cheeks and into her ears.

She looked off to the side. Toward the other flowering patch. Twisting her eyes over took all the effort she could muster. The strain was almost unbearable. Her eyes felt like they'd rip out of her skull if she looked too long. Hazel, Roth, and Jack were all perfectly still. But. . . What would she actually see were she to peel back their lids and look into their eyes? If they were still living, if they—

"I can't let you go. Not again. I need you, Sophy. I need your love and your magic here beside me. We have to be together. All of us. Don't you see?" He twisted his head to look up at her. "It's better this way." Shaking fingers crept up her neck until they squeezed her face.

Then he kissed her. "This is what we need. We all just need to stay here. You'll see soon enough. It's better this way. We have all the time in the world."

Moonrise

Sheri Yutzy

Noona was born in the air.

Her mother had gambled her last coins on a crop of thistlewort, and when the crop failed, she had nothing left to buy the spell to keep her grounded during moonrise. She had bound herself to a hemlock trunk and brought Noona into the waking world with air beneath her legs.

It seemed fitting that now, eighteen autumns later, Noona found herself clinging to a branch on the edge of Thelasse Grove.

The air glittered like knives, filled with the moonlight's power. Every breath she inhaled tugged her body higher, until her limbs shook with the strain of clutching the hemlock branch. "You have the moon's blood, darling," Mother had always said.

Noona cursed as her fingers began to cramp where they dug into a crack in the bark.

"Let go, Noona. . ." a voice crooned from the forest floor. The trees swayed in the night breeze, their leaves casting fluttering shadows across the ground.

Noona's skin crawled as she glanced down at the figure wrapped in a dark cloak. How had the Sorceress found her?

"She is calling to you." The Sorceress edged into the moonlight and tossed her long hair back, letting the light strike her pale cheeks. Her eyes were dead black, reflecting nothing. The polished handle of her staff gleamed.

"What do you mean?" Noona's voice sounded like it came out of a long funnel, the kind you poured poison down when you were mixing a brew for someone who had done you wrong.

"It is time for you to go to her." The Sorceress moved back into darkness and raised her arms. The night breeze rose from her staff, then swelled into a swirling wind. The hemlock Noona clung to groaned, and gusts tossed her body against the trunk. The jagged bark dug into her back. Her aching fingers slipped and she forced them to a new grip on the branch.

"Stop!" she grunted through her teeth. "Leave me be."

"I cannot." The Sorceress always sounded as if she were beginning an incantation. "She requires a sacrifice. You are the one that will cost Thelasse the least."

If she hadn't been clutching the branch for her life, Noona would have clutched her belly and laughed. Of course she would be chosen as a sacrifice. An orphan lurking at the edges of polite village society. Pretty enough to steal a few kisses from the Sorceress's son, but never good enough to be safe here.

Just like her mother.

"Let the moon take you," the Sorceress hissed.

"Why should I?" Indignation fed warmth into her arms, now nearly numb from her grip and the blasts of air. "Thelasse has never extended a hand to me, that I would want to give myself for her. She has given me nothing but broken promises." Noona said this last with scorn, her eyes seeking the Sorceress in the shadows.

When she had gone to the Sorceress to beg for the moonrise spell because she could not bear one more night pressed against a cold cave ceiling, the Sorceress had laughed and told her no useless girl who seduced her son's heart would receive the spell. Furthermore, she would never see Mica again.

A thought struck her and she shifted. Her grip slipped and one leg ripped free, caught in the moon's relentless pull.

The Sorceress dropped her arms. "Mica will be free, and Thelasse will be stronger for it."

"Free to cower before you," Noona forced out. Everything cramped now, and she was beginning to wonder if letting the moon swallow her alive would really be so bad.

But something else tugged at her now, a niggling

memory that hid at the edge of her mind. "You have the moon's blood, darling," her mother had said.

Mother had only shrugged when Noona asked what it meant. The moonrise had always been stronger for her. Others could simply tie themselves to their beds inside and pass an uncomfortable night without the moonrise spell. Noona spent every moonrise in agony, pressed so hard against whatever lay between her and the moon that she wore its imprints for days. And it grew worse every year.

What if the Sorceress was right? Was she so connected to the moon that it was hopeless to resist? She sighed and her body relaxed slightly, her grip slipping again. Noona scrabbled for a new hold as the Sorceress chanted encouraging yet sinister lines about letting the air take her.

Her fingers caught on a knob of wood and she reeled herself back to the branch. She reached around to clasp her wrist but the Sorceress flung both hands into the air, sending a wave of frigid air slamming into her.

The grit of hemlock bark fell away and she floated in moonlight.

The sharp air pierced her like tiny pins and she screamed. She spread her arms wide, glaring at the dark ground below, and willed herself to stop.

"The moon is sinking," the Sorceress snarled, wincing as she stepped fully into the prickling light.

Noona dared to glance up. The moon's pale face had

indeed moved toward the horizon. She focused on the ground again and pulled herself down. It felt like swimming deep in a midnight pool, slow and heavy, unnatural.

The Sorceress howled, gashing a tree trunk with her staff. "No! You are bringing her down."

The moon followed Noona all the way to the ground, hovering over the distant horizon. The Sorceress flung gales at her, ice storms, clods of dirt, but nothing slowed her inexorable descent. Her feet firmly planted in the bracken. She lifted her chin. The Sorceress had paused, panting, her staff braced against the ground before her.

"Perhaps I was not the desired sacrifice after all," Noona said coolly.

A dry male laugh rolled out of the trees behind her. She sighed, an affectionate smile teasing her lips. "That took you long enough," she called to Mica. "What did you do, get a splinter breaking out of the tower?"

The Sorceress spat a curse, but Noona, steady and still in her newfound power, felt no fear.

"She locked me in the dungeon," Mica said, strolling to stand beside her. His tenor voice sounded as jaunty as ever, like he was telling jokes in the tavern rather than interrupting a confrontation between a Sorceress and her would-be prey. Noona scanned his immaculate tunic and hosiery. Had he kept himself that neat in the dungeon, or had he changed before coming to find her? "Mother, it appears we have a new Sorceress in Thelasse."

Noona and the Sorceress both frowned, Noona's born of confusion. "What do you mean?"

"You led the moon to its resting place. That is meant to be the Sorceress's job, is it not?" He stepped closer to the Sorceress, who pretended to brush dirt from her cloak. When she didn't respond, he turned back to Noona. "Mother has never been able to do it. I think she was hoping sacrificing you would keep the moon sated enough to lessen its pull on everyone else."

"There has not been a moon guide in a century," the Sorceress spat. "The last sacrifice worked well enough."

Noona narrowed her eyes. "Last sacrifice?"

The Sorceress waved a hand. "She will only take a certain kind of person, an outcast. That was why I chose—"

Without realizing it, Noona strode forward until she stood close enough to see the Sorceress's eyes clearly. They weren't flat black now. They held something fearful at the edges. "My mother."

Cold anger trickled through her. Her mother hadn't disappeared, abandoned her, like the whispers said. She'd been taken.

Noona lifted her hands, feeling the glittering power of the moon far behind her. Its sharpness pricked her fingers, and she reveled in how fierce it felt.

She could send it forward like a wave, pierce her

mother's murderer a thousand times and leave her bleeding black on the forest floor. The Sorceress stumbled, lifting her staff back up as if to ward her off.

Noona pictured her mother, floating helplessly up and up until she was only a speck on the moon's face.

With a howl she cast the moon's shards and a crack resounded across the grove. The Sorceress lay huddled on the ground, her staff broken in pieces around her. She twitched, then lifted her head, eyes wide. When she saw Noona still staring at her, she scurried up and fled into the forest.

Mica stirred at her side. "You could have killed her." He almost sounded disappointed.

"Yes," Noona said, taking his hand. "But she's your mother. And. . ." She turned and watched as the moon, released from her hold, slipped fully behind the trees, below the horizon. Mica squeezed her fingers tightly in the sudden dark. "My mother always loved the moon. Why hate the person who put her there?"

She sensed Mica's bemused smile growing, and it made her feel shy. The songs of night birds returned, filling the air with soft sweetness as she led the way back to her little cabin at the far edge of Thelasse.

"What will you do now?" he asked softly as they paused on the threshold.

Noona opened the door and closed her eyes at the familiar scent of lavender that hung in bundles from the ceiling. "Sleep until the next moonrise," she said, laughing.

She would sleep soundly, knowing Mother was up there, waiting for her to return.

He leaned against the door, his eyes gleaming with unabashed affection. "Would you like company?"

Trees

Denica McCall

Beams of gold-flecked light sift through the trees as if through a sieve
    Reflecting the hidden glow in my soul
  It pulses like a heart, a candle in the dark, as I
  Weave through this mysterious forest at the birth of dusk
  And I'm learning how to trust, forging a way through this dirt at my feet,
  Seeing how I was made from such things
  But knowing eternity rushes in my veins, like
  The wings overhead, how they cut through the air
  How those lungs screech through the quiet, invite a sense of depth
  That creates heights like the cliff before my eyes
  I stop,
  Breathe,
  Take in the scene before me, no longer in my periphery

The House Built Between the Branches

The edge, it calls to me

To leap and know I'll make it back home, I'll have ample time to

Explore the maze of the trees behind me, it

Blinds me, this fear, this trepidation at what I think I'll lose

But I won't if I just

Trust you

Another day, another page, another part of the story, I think

If I wait, maybe

Then your hand slips in, encloses mine in warmth

As branches dance in wild wind, and I face north, every nerve under my skin

Lifted,

Fire ignited, dashing through each limb until my heart finds its peace

On the ends of your words

Your rumoring lips are my air now, and I'm off the rim of this jarring fear now,

I am free

And these trees, they wave your melody, a backdrop to my flight, my

Cave opens wide, until light displaces the fight

I was made for this beauty, to reach beyond the night

At the cusp of dusk, your presence is fresh light

About the Authors

Authors listed in story order.
Please be sure to read all the following author bios
and give them a follow!
Additionally, please be sure to note which stories
were your favorite, and which scared you the most, in a
review anywhere reviews can be posted.

Willow Whitehead

Willow Whitehead has a love/hate relationship with writing, the words will spill onto the page faster than she can type, or she'll stare at a blank document for hours. Though the words always come a bit easier in the middle of the night. Currently she spends her days drinking tea, haunting the shelves of her local library, and hiking through the woods. You can follow her on Instagram @weepingwillowreviews, and watch as she struggles to balance her time between work, rest, and her innumerable hobbies.

Her previous publications include The Willow Tree Swing, Of Ink and Paper, and Balloon Children.

Emma Lovejoy

Emma Lovejoy is an author and historian in Boston. They strive to see the magic in ordinary things, and love uncovering untold and under-appreciated stories. Their writing time at present is largely consumed by their M.A. thesis, with a research focus on circus and sideshow history. However, they make time for their fictional work whenever they can.

Danni Grace

Danni Grace is an author who finds no greater joy than sending her characters on fantastical, whimsical, and perhaps harrowing adventures. She loves the world of literature like it's her own home, and there is nothing she would want to do more than write. When she's not writing, she can be found curled up on the couch with her chihuahua and muse, Gidget, or diving headfirst into a new spontaneous hobby.

Anne J. Hill

Anne J. Hill is an author who enjoys writing fantasy for all ages. Her love of words has led to her career as an editor and content writer. She runs Twenty Hills Publishing with the help of her circus-performing best friend, Lara E. Madden. She spends her days dreaming up fantastical realms, researching ways to get away with murder…for writing, arguing over commas at the kitchen table, talking out loud to the characters in her head, promising her housemate that she isn't, in fact, crazy, and rearranging her personal library—affectionately dubbed the "Book Dungeon."

Instagram @anne.j.hill.editing

www.annejhill.com

Mia Dalia

Mia Dalia is an internationally published, CWA-nominated author of all things fantastic, thrilling, scary, and strange. Her tales of horror, noir, science fiction, mystery, crime, humor, and more have been featured in a variety of anthologies, magazines, literary journals, online, and adapted for narrative podcasts.

Her stories have been voted top ten of Tales to Terrify 2023 and shortlisted for the CWA's Daggers Awards 2024. She is the author of the novels Estate Sale and Haven; novellas, Tell Me a Story, Discordant, and Arrokoth; and the collection, Smile So Red and Other Tales of Madness.

daliaverse.wixsite.com/author

linktr.ee/daliaverse

Hailey Huntington

Hailey Huntington is a speculative fiction author, penning tales of wonder, hope, and heroes, with a dash of wit. Her stories can be found online and in various print anthologies. You can connect with her on Instagram and Facebook: @haileyhuntingtonauthor
or her website: haileyhuntington.com

Abraham Vila

Abraham Vila, 23 years old and originally from Spain, is a graduate in English Studies from the Complutense University of Madrid (UCM). He holds an MA in American Studies from UCM and an MA in Modern Languages from the University of Nebraska-Lincoln (UNL). His current research focuses on Native American literature and mythology, exploring how these elements intertwine to shape narratives of resistance and protest in contemporary contexts. He has already published several books of poems. He loves autumn, cats, and rainy days with coffee. He plays the saxophone and likes music, cinema and art in general.

Karissa Riffel

Karissa Riffel is a wife, mom, and English teacher. Her short fiction has appeared in various literary magazines. Her nonfiction has appeared on the Rabbit Room blog and is forthcoming by the Anselm Society and CiRCE Press. She is co-host of the podcast Lit Ladies, and she writes about art and faith on her Substack Midnight Ink. When she isn't writing, you can find her drinking pots of tea and re-reading Jane Eyre.

She can be found on Instagram as @karissariffel.books

Effie Joe Stock

Effie Joe Stock is the author of The Shadows of Light series, creator of the world Rasa, and head of Dragon Bone Publishing. When she's not slaving away in front of her computer, you can find her playing music, studying psychology, theology, or philosophy, playing fantasy RPG video games, riding motorcycles, or hanging out with her farm animals. Her publishing journey only just beginning, Stock looks forward to the release of the rest of her fantasy series along with other Dragon Bone titles.

Anayis N. Der Hakopian

Anayis N. Der Hakopian is a Visual Storyteller and Creative Researcher based in London (UK) where she crafts folkish and eerie narratives for the screen, page and stage. When she isn't stuck behind a computer screen she spends her free time writing poetry in the park whilst being mobbed by dogs.

Hannah Carter

Hannah Carter is the author of stories filled with mermaids, magic, and murder. Her novels include The Atlantis trilogy and the short story collection Saltwater Souls. In her spare time, you can find her snuggling her cats, drinking a copious amount of tea, or listening to Taylor Swift. Follow her at Instagram on @mermaidhannahwrites or her website www.authorhannahcarter.com.

Vanessa E. Howard

Vanessa E. Howard writes primarily fantasy for young adult and middle grade. She has been a newspaper reporter, magazine writer, and college composition teacher. A member of the Flash Fiction Magic and Realm Makers communities, she is also a homeschool mom and co-op teacher. Her short fiction has been published by Spark, Havok, Twenty Hills, and Quill and Flame. Ms. Howard lives with her family in Central Texas.

She can be found on Instagram as writervanessa, Facebook as Vanessa E. Howard-Writer, and at her website vanessaehoward.com.

K. DeCristofaro

K. DeCristofaro is a poet and multidisciplinary artist living in Boston, Massachusetts with her cat, dog, and partner. She is a hobbyist green witch, an herbal tea devotee, a horror film enthusiast, and a joyfully queer force of nature. Her work can be found in publications by Humana Obscura, Querencia Press, Beyond Queer Words, and Nightshade Publishing, and more. Her Horror-themed poetry chapbook, Why I'm Watching, is available from Bottlecap Press. Find K. on Instagram at @herbalteapoetry.

AudraKate Gonzalez

AudraKate Gonzalez started writing horror stories when she ran out of Goosebumps books to read as a child. Her love for horror grew and now she has a BA in Creative Writing and is working on her MFA. She is a current member of the Horror Writer's Association, and The International English Honor Society (Sigma Tau Delta). The award winning first book (Tomato Juice) in her Young Adult Horror series (This is Noir) is available now. You can read more of her short stories in anthologies published by Twenty Hills Publishing, and Aphotic Realm. AudraKate lives in Ohio with her handsome husband, and her adorable furry bad boys, Zero and Scrappy Doo. When AudraKate isn't writing, you can find her reading, watching scary movies or sleeping. You can follow her on Instagram and TikTok: @lets.get.lit.erature

Julia Skinner

Julia Skinner is a nineteen-year-old, modern day hobbit, with a love for good stories and chocolate ice cream. She lives in South Texas with her family and two miniature Australian Shepherds (and a ton of other animals). When she's not working on one of her many fantasy novels or flash fictions, she can be found juggling college, playing video games, dreaming up yet another entrepreneurial project, or happy-ranting about Brandon Sanderson's books. She is a sinner saved by Jesus, and if any good comes from her journey, it's because of Him.

Her published works include Prismatic, Fool's Honor, Casting Call, Darkness & Moonlight, and more! You can join her on her writing journey over on Instagram @ litaflameblog

Nathaniel Luscombe

Nathaniel Luscombe is an up-and-coming author from Ontario, Canada. He is best known for Moon Soul and The Planets We Become, and has also been in a handful of anthologies. He fills his time with a full-time job, lots of book ideas, and the responsibilities that come with co-running Dragon Bone Publishing.

Xanna Renae

Xanna Renae loves daydreaming about how to save her characters from the messes she puts them in. Currently she is giving life to the ideas inside her head from rural Missouri where she lives with her husband, Noah, and cat, Calcifer. She has a BA in Creative Writing from Southern New Hampshire University, where she graduated Summa Cum Laude. When she isn't writing you can find her tucked away in her little bungalow reading, snuggling with her cat, or playing video games with her husband.

Her published works include her debut fantasy novel *Down with the Prince*, and Nightshade's *Balloon Children, Of Ink & Paper, The Willow Tree Swing,* and her personal collection of short stories and poems: *Through the Violet Redwoods.* Find her online pretty much everywhere @XannasBooks or on her website: XannaRenae.com

Sheri Yutzy

Hi, I'm Sheri Yutzy. I love forests under the night sky, trying new foods, and drinking Irish tea. I've been to 21 countries, and once spent the night in a hotel lobby in Florence, Italy, because the entire city was fully booked for a festival. I'm married to a musician who looks good in black, mama to four kids, and happy resident of a Cape Cod cottage in Ohio. I write atmospheric fantasy and am acquisitions editor at sparkflashfiction.com. Join my email list for publishing updates, free fiction, & recipes!

Denica McCall

Denica McCall is a young adult fantasy writer, poet, dreamer, and deep thinker who grew up in the Pacific Northwest and now resides in Kansas City. When not writing, she works as a nanny and a freelance editor. She also enjoys attending dance classes, visiting coffee shops, and planning her next travel adventure. She is currently working on her third YA novel which features fairies, a pegasus, and cave-stars.

Find out more and sign up for her newsletter to receive a free short story at denicamccall.com

On Instagram: @denicamcauthor

Or on Facebook: @denicamccallwriter

Nightshade Publishing®

Nightshade Publishing® was founded in 2019 by Xanna Renae. In 2022 Willow Whitehead joined the team as a co-founder.

Nightshade's goal is to publish the stories that inspire the beauty in chaos. We are your writer apothecary, providing your every bookish need. Built for the readers who want to feel like they're walking through a haunted wood with a friend by their side, telling them a story to get them through the dark and into a glowing meadow.